TELLING STORIES

A. L. BARKER
MAEVE BINCHY
CHRISTOPHER BURNS
MICHAEL CARSON
ANGELA CARTER
MARY FLANAGAN
JANE GARDAM
ROMESH GUNESEKERA
CHRISTOPHER HOPE
JOHN McGAHERN
DEBORAH MOGGACH
RICHARD NELSON
FREDERIC RAPHAEL
MICHELE ROBERTS
DILYS ROSE
GREG SNOW
D. J. TAYLOR
JONATHAN TREITEL
LYNNE TRUSS

Telling Stories

The best of BBC Radio's recent short fiction

Edited by Duncan Minshull

Title story by Maeve Binchy

CORONET
Hodder and Stoughton

This collection first published in Great Britain in 1992 as a Coronet paperback original

Introduction and compilation copyright © 1992 Duncan Minshull

For copyright in individual stories see page v

British Library CIP

Telling stories: The best of BBC Radio's recent short fiction.
I. Minshull, Duncan
823[F]

ISBN 0-340-56454-7

Printed and bound in Great Britain for Hodder and Stoughton Paperbacks, a division of Hodder and Stoughton Ltd, Mill Road, Dunton Green, Sevenoaks, Kent TN13 2YA. (Editorial Office: 47 Bedford Square, London WC1B 3DP) by Clays Ltd, St Ives plc, Bungay, Suffolk. Photoset by Rowland Phototypesetting Ltd, Bury St Edmunds, Suffolk.

ACKNOWLEDGEMENTS

CONTENTS

INTRODUCTION

Eighteen of the twenty stories that make up this collection were written specially for BBC Radio and selected from a range of London and regional work broadcast between 1990 and early 1991. This is the first time that any of them have appeared in book form.

The choice was made from the two networks that do most to support original writing. The great provider has been Radio 4's fifteen-minute *Morning Story*, now broadcasting in the afternoons as *Short Story*. And then there is Radio 3. No fixed duration here, so the listener (and now the reader) can enjoy stories more varied in length. It has also been enjoyable to liaise with various publications on joint commissions. *Cosmopolitan*, the now departed *Listener* and the *Weekend Guardian* have all published stories to tie in with broadcast on one of the two networks.

Producing short fiction for radio always raises the question: what qualities do stories written for the ear share with those destined for the page? Well, perhaps the answer is simply more of the same. Listen to a story and you are unable to go back and recoup your thoughts; no opportunity to ponder the convoluted plot or intricate description. More of the same means that the radio story has to have even greater clarity and directness. It has to provide the situation, the character, the mood, that fragment of life, even more quickly or the audience will turn off. Every word has to work.

These twenty stories aim to show the fragment of life to be as varied and surprising as possible. Radio, we never tire of suggesting, can convey a palpable picture of anywhere at any time through the precision of the writing; then it's up to the listener to develop their own mental pictures. Nights at the circus, days in a Japanese cinema, Christmas in Borneo, Atlantic crossings and French kitchens all figure in the following pages. And as varied are the contributors themselves. Stories continue to be popular on radio because the best practitioners continue to write for us and I am delighted that so many are included here. But it is equally satisfying to feature those who are established but fairly new to the medium: Christopher Hope, Jane Gardam and Mary Flanagan. There is a first story by the American playwright Richard Nelson and a crop of tales by such under-35 talents as Jonathan Treitel, D. J. Taylor, Greg Snow and Romesh Gunesekera. And the novelist Michael Carson has two pieces included. His is a prolific broadcasting record, with over twenty-five stories for Radio 4.

The obvious pleasure in putting together *Telling Stories* is to work with material that delights both ear and eye. It has also come about through the repeated requests of our radio audience. So, if we can please the listener and put a distinctive collection in the bookshops, then it has been a job well done.

Good reading!

Duncan Minshull
Stories Editor, BBC Radio
September 1991

LIZZIE'S TIGER

Angela Carter

Angela Carter's work includes *Nights at the Circus*, the story collection *Black Venus* and the essay anthology *Nothing Sacred*. Her latest novel is *Wise Children*. She lives in London.

'Lizzie's Tiger' was first broadcast on Radio 3, read by Liza Ross.

When the circus came to town and Lizzie saw the tiger, they were living on Ferry Street, in a very poor way. It was the time of the greatest parsimony in their father's house. Everyone knows the first hundred thousand is the most difficult and the dollar bills were breeding slowly, slowly, even if he practised a little touch of usury on the side to prick his cash in the direction of greater productivity. In another ten years' time, the War between the States would provide rich pickings for the coffin-makers, but, back then, back in the fifties, well – if he had been a praying man, he would have gone down on his knees for a little outbreak of summer cholera or a touch of typhoid. To the father's chagrin, there had been nobody to bill when he had buried his wife.

For, at that time, the girls were just freshly orphaned. Emma was thirteen and Lizzie four – stern and square, a squat rectangle of a child. Emma parted Lizzie's hair in the middle, stretched it back over each side of her bulging forehead and braided it tight. Emma dressed her, undressed her, scrubbed her night and morning with a damp flannel, and humped the great lump of little girl around in her arms whenever Lizzie would let her, although Lizzie was not a demonstrative child and did not show affection easily, except to the head of the house, and then only when she wanted something. She knew where the power was and, intuitively feminine in spite of her gruff appearance, she knew how to court it.

That cottage on Ferry – well, it was a slum; but the undertaker lived on unconcerned among the stiff furnishings of his defunct marriage. His bits and pieces would be admired today if they turned up freshly beeswaxed in an antique store, but in those days they were plain old-fashioned, and time would only make them more so in that dreary interior. The tiny house he never mended, eroding clapboard and diseased paint, mildew on the dark wallpaper with a brown pattern like brains, the ominous crimson border round the top of the

3

walls, the sisters sleeping in one room in one thrifty bed.

On Ferry, in the worst part of town, among the dark-skinned Portuguese fresh off the boat with their earrings, flashing teeth and incomprehensible speech, come over the ocean to work the mills, those newly-erected chimneys closed in every perspective, every year more chimneys, more smoke, more newcomers, and the peremptory shriek of the whistle that summoned to labour as bells had once summoned to prayer.

The hovel on Ferry stood, or, rather, leaned at a bibulous angle on a narrow street cut across at an oblique angle by another narrow street. All the old wooden homes looked like an upset cookie jar of broken gingerbread houses lurching this way and that way: the shutters hanging off their hinges and windows stuffed with old newspapers and the snagged picket fence and raised voices in unknown tongues and howling of dogs who, since puppyhood, had known of the world only the circumference of their chain. Outside the parlour window were nothing but rows of counterfeit houses that sometimes used to scream.

Such was the anxious architecture of the two girls' early childhood.

A hand came in the night and stuck a poster, showing the head of a tiger, onto a picket fence. As soon as Lizzie saw the poster, she wanted to go to the circus. But Emma had no money, not a cent. The thirteen-year-old was keeping house at that time. The last skivvy had just quit with bad words on both sides. Every morning, Father would compute the day's expenses, hand Emma just so much, no more. He was angry when he saw the poster on his fence. He thought the circus should have paid him rental for the use. He came home in the evening, sweet with embalming fluid, saw the poster, purpled with fury, ripped it off, tore it up.

Then it was supper-time. Emma was no great shakes at cookery and Father, dismissing the possibility of another costly skivvy until such time as plague struck, already pondered the cost-efficiency of remarriage. When Emma served up her hunks of cod, translucently uncooked within, her

4

warmed-over coffee and a dank loaf of baker's bread, it almost put him in a courting mood. But that is not to say his meal improved his temper. So that, when his youngest climbed kitten-like upon his knee and, lisping, twining her tiny fingers in his gunmetal watch-chain, begged small change for the circus, he answered her with words of unusual harshness, for he truly loved this last daughter, whose obduracy recalled his own.

Emma unhandily darned a sock.

'Get that child to bed before I lose my temper!'

Emma dropped the sock and scooped up Lizzie, whose mouth set in dour lines of affront as she was borne off. The square-jawed scrap deposited on the rustling straw mattress – oat straw, softest and cheapest – saw where she had been dropped and stared at the dust in a sunbeam. She seethed with resentment. It was moist midsummer, only six o'clock and still bright day outside.

But she had a whim of iron, this one. She swung her feet on to the stool upon which the girls climbed down out of bed, thence to the floor. The kitchen door stood open for air behind the screen door. From the parlour came the low murmur of Emma's voice as she read *The Providence Journal* aloud to Father.

Next door's lean and famished hound launched itself at the fence in a frenzy of yapping that concealed the creak of Lizzie's boots on the back porch. Unobserved, she was off – off and away – trotting down Ferry Street, her cheeks pink with self-reliance and intent. She would not be denied. The circus! The word tinkled in her head with a red sound, as if it might signify a profane church.

'That's a tiger,' Emma had told her as, hand in hand, they inspected the poster on their fence.

'A tiger is a big cat,' Emma added instructively.

How big a cat?

A *very* big cat.

A dumpy, red-striped, regular cat of the small, domestic variety greeted Lizzie with a raucous mew from atop a gatepost as she stumped determinedly along Ferry Street.

It was Ginger, whom Emma, in a small ecstasy of sentimental whimsy would sometimes call 'Miss Ginger', or even, 'Miss Ginger Cuddles'. Lizzie, however, sternly ignored Miss Ginger Cuddles. Miss Ginger Cuddles sneaked. The cat put out a paw as Lizzie brushed past, as if seeking to detain her, as if to suggest she took second thoughts as to her escapade. But, for all the apparent decision with which Lizzie put one firm foot before the other, she had not the least idea where the circus might be, and would not have got there at all without the help of a gaggle of ragged Irish children from Corkey Row, who happened by in the company of a lean, black and tan, barking dog of unforeseen breed.

This free-ranging dog with its easy-going grin took a fancy to Lizzie and, yapping with glee, danced around the little figure in the white pinafore as it marched along. Lizzie reached out to pat its head. She was a fearless girl.

The child-gang saw her pet their dog and took a fancy to her for the same reason as crows settle on one particular tree. Their wild smiles circled round her. 'Going to the circus, are ye? See the clown and the ladies dancing?' Lizzie knew nothing about clowns and dancers, but she nodded, and one boy took hold of one hand, another of the other, so they raced her off between them. They soon saw her little legs could not keep up their pace, so the ten-year-old put her up on his shoulders where she rode like a lord. Soon they came to a field on the edge of town.

'See the Big Top?' There was a red and white striped tent of scarcely imaginable proportions, into which you could have popped the entire house on Ferry, and the yard too, with enough room to spare inside for another house, and another. A vast red and white striped tent, with ripping naphtha flares outside and, besides this, all manner of other tents, booths and stalls, dotted about the field. But most of all Lizzie was impressed by the great number of people, for it seemed to her that the whole town must be out tonight. Yet, when you looked closely at the throng, there was no one who looked like she did, or her father did, or Emma.

Nowhere that old New England lantern jaw, those ice-blue eyes.

She was a stranger among these strangers. For here were those the mills had brought to town, the ones with different faces. The plump, pink-cheeked Lancashire mill-hands, with brave red neckerchiefs; the sombre features of the Canucks imbibing fun with characteristic gloom; and the white smiles of the Portuguese, who knew how to enjoy themselves, laughter tripping off their tipsy-sounding tongues.

'Here y'are!' announced her random companions as they dumped her down and, feeling they had amply done their duty by their self-imposed charge, they capered off among the throng, planning, perhaps, to slither under the canvas and so enjoy the shows for free, or even to pick a pocket or two to complete the treat, who knows?

Above the field, the sky now acquired the melting tones of the end of the day: the plush, smoky sunsets unique to these unprecedented industrial cities, sunsets never seen in this world before the Age of Steam that set the mills in motion that made us all modern.

At sunset, the incomparably grave and massive light of New England acquires a monumental, a Roman sensuality. Under this sternly voluptuous sky, Lizzie abandoned herself to the unpremeditated smells and never-before-heard noises – hot fat in a vat of frying doughnuts; horsedung; boiling sugar; frying onions; popping corn; vomit; sweat; cries of vendors; crack of rifles from the range; singsong of the white-faced clown, who clattered a banjo, while a woman in pink fleshings danced upon a little stage. Too much for Lizzie to take in at once. Too much for Lizzie to take in at all. Too rich a feast for her senses, so that she was taken a little beyond herself and felt her head spinning, a vertigo, a sense of profound strangeness overcoming her.

Unnoticeably small as she was, she was taken up by the crowd and tossed about among insensitive shoes and petticoats. Too close to the ground to see much else for long, she imbibed the frenetic bustle of the midway through her nose, her ears, her skin that twitched, prickled, heated up with excitement so that she began to colour up in the way she had, her cheeks marked with red, like the marbling on the insides of the family Bible. She found herself swept by the tide of the crowd to a long table where hard cider was sold from a barrel.

The white tablecloth was wet and sticky with spillage and gave forth a dizzy, sweet, metallic odour. An old woman filled tin mugs at the barrel spigot, mug after mug, and threw coins onto other coins in a tin box – splash, chink, clang. Lizzie clung on to the edge of the table to prevent herself being carried away again. Splash, chink, clang. Trade was brisk, so the old woman never turned the spigot off and cider cascaded onto the ground on the other side of the table.

The devil got into Lizzie, then. She ducked down and sneaked in under the edge of the tablecloth, to hide in the resonant darkness and crouch on the crushed grass in fresh mud. She held out her hands under the discontinuous stream from the spigot until she collected two hollowed palmsfuls, which she licked up, and smacked her lips. Filled, licked, smacked again. She was so preoccupied with her delicious thievery that she jumped half out of her skin when she felt a living, quivering thing thrust into her neck in that very sensitive spot where her braids divided. Something moist and intimate shoved inquisitively at the nape of her neck.

She craned round and came face to face with a melancholy piglet, decently dressed in a slightly soiled ruff. She courteously filled her palms with cider and offered it to her new acquaintance, who sucked it up eagerly. She squirmed to feel the wet quiver of the pig's curious lips against her hands. It drank, tossed its pink snout, and trotted off out the back way from the table.

Lizzie did not hesitate. She followed the piglet past the dried-cod smell of the cider-seller's skirts. The piglet's tail disappeared beneath a cart piled with fresh barrels that was pulled up behind the stall. Lizzie pursued the engaging piglet to find herself suddenly out in the open again, but this time in an abrupt margin of pitch black and silence. She had slipped out of the circus grounds through a hole in their periphery and the dark had formed into a huge clot, the night, whilst Lizzie was underneath the table; behind her the lights were, but here only shadowy undergrowth, stirring, and then the call of a night bird.

The pig paused to rootle the earth. But when Lizzie reached out to stroke it, it shook its ears out of its eyes and took off at a great pace into the countryside. However, her attention was immediately diverted from this disappointment by the sight of a man who stood with his back to the lights, leaning slightly forward. The cider-barrel spigot sound repeated itself. Fumbling with the front of his trousers, he turned round and tripped over Lizzie, because he was a little unsteady on his feet and she was scarcely to be seen among the shadows. He bent down and took hold of her shoulders.

'Small child,' he said, and belched a puff of acridity into her face. Lurching a little, he squatted right down in front of her, so they were on the same level. It was so dark that she could see of his face only the hint of a moustache above the pale half-moon of his smile.

'Small girl,' he corrected himself, after a closer look. He did not speak like ordinary folks. He was not from around these parts. He belched again, and tugged at his trousers. He took firm hold of her right hand and brought it tenderly up between his squatting thighs.

'Small girl, do you know what *this* is for?'

She felt buttons; serge; something hairy; something moist and moving. She didn't mind it. He kept his hand on hers and made her rub him for a minute or two. He hissed between his teeth: 'Kissy. Kissy from missy?'

She minded that and shook an obdurate head. She did not like her father's hard, dry, imperative kisses, and endured them only for the sake of power. Sometimes Emma touched her cheek lightly with unparted lips. Lizzie would allow no more. The man sighed when she shook her head, took her hand away from his crotch, softly folded it up on its fingers and gave her hand ceremoniously back to her.

'Gratuity,' he said, felt in his pocket and flipped her a nickel. Then he straightened up and walked away. Lizzie put

9

the coin in her pinafore pocket and, after a moment's thought, stumped off after the funny man along the still, secret edges of the field, curious as to what he might do next.

But now surprises were going on all round her in the bushes: mewings, squeaks, rustlings, although the funny man paid no attention to them, not even when a stately fat woman rose up under his feet: huge as a moon and stark except for her stays, and black cotton stockings held up by garters with silk rosettes on them, and a majestic hat of black leghorn with feathers. The woman addressed the drunken man angrily, in a language with a good many k's in it. But he ploughed on indifferently and Lizzie scuttled unseen after, casting an inquisitive backward glance. She had never seen a woman's naked breasts since she could remember. And this pair of melons jiggled entrancingly as the fat woman shook her fist in the wake of the funny man – before she parted her thighs with a wet smack and sank down on her knees again in the grass in which something unseen moaned.

Then a person scarcely as tall as Lizzie herself, dressed up like a little drummer-boy, somersaulted – head-over-heels – directly across their paths, muttering to himself as he did so. Lizzie had just the time to see that. Although he was small, he was not shaped quite right. His head seemed to have been pressed into his shoulders with some violence. But then he was gone.

Don't think any of this frightened her. She was not the kind of child that frightens easily.

Then they were at the back of a tent. Not the big, striped tent, but another, smaller tent, where the funny man fumbled with the flap much as he had fumbled with his trousers. A bright mauve, ammoniac reek pulsed out from this tent. It was lit up inside like a Chinese lantern and glowed. At last he managed to unfasten and went inside. He did not attempt to close up after him; he seemed to be in as great a hurry as the tumbling dwarf – so Lizzie slipped through too, but as soon as she was inside, she lost him, because there were so many other people there.

Feet of customers had worn all the grass from the ground

and it had been replaced by sawdust, which soon stuck all over the mudpie Lizzie had become. The tent was lined with cages on wheels, but she could not see high enough to see what was inside them, yet, mixed with the everyday chatter around her, she heard strange cries that did not come from human throats, so she knew she was on the right track.

She saw what could be seen: a young couple, arm in arm, he whispering in her ear, she giggling. A group of three grinning, gaping youths, poking sticks within the bars. A family that went down in steps of size, a man, a woman, a boy, a girl, a boy, a girl, a boy, a girl, down to a baby of indeterminate sex in the woman's arms. There were many more present, but these were the people she took account of.

The gagging stench was worse than a summer privy and a savage hullabaloo went on all the time, a roaring as if the sea had teeth.

She eeled her way past skirts and trousers and scratched bare legs of summer boys until she was standing beside the biggest brother of the staircase family at the front of the crowd, but still she could not see the tiger. Even if she stood on tiptoe, she saw only wheels and the red and gold base of the cage, whereon was depicted a woman without any clothes, much like the one in the grass outside only without the hat and stockings, and some foliage, with a gilded moon and stars. The brother of the staircase family was much older than she, perhaps twelve, and clearly of the lower class, but clean and respectable-looking, although the entire family possessed that pale, peculiar look characteristic of the mill operatives. The brother looked down and saw a small child in a filthy pinafore peering and straining upwards.

'*Veux-tu voir le chat grand, ma petite?*'

Lizzie did not understand what he said, but she knew what he was saying and nodded assent. Mother looked over the head of the good baby in the lace bonnet as her son heaved Lizzie up in his arms for a good look.

'*Les poux . . .*' she warned, but her son paid her no heed.

'*Voilà, ma petite!*'

The tiger walked up and down, up and down. It walked

up and down like Satan walking about the world and it burned. It burned so brightly, she was scorched. Its tail, thick as her father's forearm, twitched back and forth at the tip. The quick, loping stride of the caged tiger; its eyes like yellow coins of a foreign currency; its round, innocent, toy-like ears; the stiff whiskers sticking out with an artificial look; the red mouth from which the bright noise came. It walked up and down on straw strewn with bloody bones.

The tiger kept its head down, questing hither and thither – though in quest of what might not be told. All its motion was slung from the marvellous haunches it held so high you could have rolled a marble down its back (if it would have let you). In its hindlegs the tense muscles keened and sang. It was a miracle of dynamic suspension. It reached one end of the cage in a few paces and whirled around upon itself in one liquid motion; nothing could be quicker or more beautiful than its walk. It was all raw, vivid, exasperated nerves. Upon its pelt it bore the imprint of the bars behind which it lived.

The young lad who kept hold of her clung tight as Lizzie lunged forward towards the beast. But he could not stop her clutching the bars of the cage with her little fingers and he tried but he could not dislodge them. The tiger stopped in its tracks halfway through its mysterious patrol and looked at her. Her pale-blue Calvinist eyes of New England encountered with a shock the flat, mineral eyes of the tiger.

It seemed to Lizzie that they exchanged this cool regard for an endless time, the tiger and herself.

Then something strange happened. The svelte beast fell to its knees. It was as if it had been subdued by the presence of this child, as if this little child of all the children in the world might lead it towards a peaceable kingdom where it need not eat meat. But only 'as if'. All we could see was, it knelt. A crackle of shock ran through the tent. The tiger was acting out of character.

Its mind remained, however, a law unto itself. We did not know what it was thinking. How could we?

It stopped roaring. Instead it started to emit a rattling purr.

Time somersaulted. All that existed in the whole world now were Lizzie and the tiger.

Then . . . it came towards her, as if she were winding it to her by the exercise of pure will. I cannot tell you how much she loved the tiger, nor how wonderful she thought it was. It was the power of her love that forced it to come to her, on its knees, like a penitent. It dragged its pale belly across the dirty straw towards the bars where the little soft creature hung by its hooked fingers. Behind it followed the serpentine length of its ceaselessly twitching tail.

There was a wrinkle in its nose and it buzzed and rumbled and they never took their eyes off one another, though neither had the least idea what the other meant.

The boy holding Lizzie got scared and pummelled her little fists, but she would not let go a grip as tight and senseless as that of the newborn.

Crack! The spell broke.

The world bounded into the ring.

A lash cracked round the tiger's carnivorous head, and a glorious hero sprang into the cage brandishing in the hand that did not hold the whip a three-legged stool. He wore fawn britches, black boots, a bright red jacket frogged with gold, a tall hat. A dervish, he; he beckoned, crouched, pointed with the whip, menaced with the stool. He leapt and twirled in a brilliant ballet of mimic ferocity, the dance of the Taming of the Tiger, to whom the tamer gave no chance to fight at all.

The great cat unpeeled its eyes off Lizzie's, rose up on its hindlegs and feinted at the whip — like our puss Ginger feints at a piece of paper dangled from a string. It batted at the tamer with its enormous paws. But the whip continued to confuse, irritate and torment and, what with the sudden, excited baying of the crowd, the tiger whimpered, laid back its ears and scampered away from the whirling man to an obscure corner of the stage — there to cower, while its flanks heaved, the picture of humiliation.

Lizzie let go of the bars and clung, mud stains and all, to her young protector for comfort. She was shaken to the roots

13

by the attack of the trainer upon the tiger and her four-year-old roots were very near the surface.

The tamer gave his whip a final, contemptuous ripple around his adversary's whiskers that made it sink its huge head on the floor. Then he placed one booted foot on the tiger's skull and cleared his throat for speech. He was a hero. He was a tiger himself, but even more so, it was because he was a man.

'Ladies and gentlemen, boys and girls, this incomparable TIGER known as the Scourge of Bengal, and brought alive-oh to Boston from its native jungle but three short months ago, now, at my imperious command, offers you a perfect imitation of docility and obedience. But do not let the brute deceive you. Brute it was, and brute it remains. Not for nothing did it receive the soubriquet of Scourge for, in its native habitat, it thought nothing of consuming a dozen brown-skinned heathen for its breakfast and followed up with a couple of dozen more for dinner!'

A pleasing shudder tingled through the crowd.

'This tiger is the veritable incarnation of bloodlust and fury. In a single instant, it can turn from furry quiescence into three hundred pounds, yes, three hundred POUNDS of death-dealing fury.

'The tiger is the cat's revenge.'

Oh, Miss Ginger, Miss Ginger Cuddles, who sat mewing censoriously on the gatepost as Lizzie passed by; who would have thought you seethed with such resentment!

The man's voice dropped to a confidential whisper and Lizzie, although she was in such a state, recognised this was the same man as the one she had met behind the cider stall. Although now he exhibited such erect mastery, and not a single person in the tent would have thought he had been drinking.

'What is the nature of the bond between us, between the Beast and Man? Let me tell you. It is fear. Nothing but fear. Do you know how insomnia is the plague of the tamer of cats? How all night long, every night, we pace our quarters, impossible to close our eyes for brooding on what day, what hour, what moment the fatal beast will choose to strike?

'Here and now I am in terror of my life.

'At this moment I am in this cage within a perfect deathtrap.'

Theatrical pause.

'But,' and here he knocked the tiger's nose with his whipstock, 'but . . .' and Lizzie saw the secret frog he kept within his trousers shift a little, '. . . BUT I'm not half so scared of the big brute as it is of me!

'For I bring to bear upon its killer instinct a rational man's knowledge of the power of fear. In my cage, among my cats, I have established a hierarchy of FEAR and among my cats you might well say I am TOP DOG, because I know that all the time they want to kill me, they just don't know what *I* might do next. No, sir!'

As if enchanted by the notion, he laughed out loud again. But by now, the tiger, perhaps incensed by the unexpected blow on the nose, rumbled out a clear message of disaffection and, with a quick jerk of its sculptured head, flung the man's foot away so that he half toppled over. And then the tiger was no longer a thing of stillness, of hard edges and clear outlines, but a whizz of black and red, maw and canines. In the air. On him.

The crowd immediately bayed.

But the tamer, with enormous presence of mind, seeing as how he was drunk, bounced backwards on his boot-heels and thrust the stool he carried in his left hand into the fierce tiger's jaws, leaving the tiger worrying, gnawing, destroying the harmless thing, as a ragged black boy quickly unlatched the cage door and out the tamer leapt, unscathed, amidst hurrahs.

Lizzie's stunned little face was now mottled all over with a curious reddish purple, with the heat of the tent, with passion, with the sudden access of enlightenment.

To see the rest of the stupendous cat act, the audience would have had to buy another ticket for the Big Top, besides the ticket for the menagerie, for which it had already paid, so, reluctant on the whole to do that, in spite of the promise of clowns and dancing ladies, it soon got bored with watching the tiger splintering the wooden stool, and drifted off.

'*Eh bien, ma petite,*' said her boy-nurse to her in a sweet, singsong, crooning voice. '*Tu a vue la bête! La bête du cauchemar!*'

The baby in the lace bonnet had slept peacefully through all this, but now began to stir and mumble. Its mother nudged her husband with her elbow.

'*On va, Papa?*'

The crooning, smiling boy brought his bright pink lips down on Lizzie's forehead for a farewell kiss. She could not bear that. She struggled furiously and shouted to be put down. With that, her cover broke and she burst out of her disguise of dirt and silence. Half the remaining gawpers in the tent had kin bleakly buried by her father. The rest owed him money. She was the most famous daughter in all Fall River.

'Well, if it ain't Andrew Borden's little girl! What are they Canucks doing with little Lizzie Borden?'

TRANSATLANTIC BLUES

Frederic Raphael

Frederic Raphael is the author of three volumes of short stories and sixteen novels including *The Limits of Love, April, June and November,* and *Heaven and Earth.* His screenplays include the Oscar-winning *Darling* and *Far from the Madding Crowd,* and his work for television includes *The Glittering Prizes, Oxbridge Blues* and *After the War.* He is currently working on a new novel, *The Field of Blood.*

'Transatlantic Blues' was first broadcast on Radio 4, read by John Rowe.

They were walking up Central Park West under a sky unscarred by frequent flight-patterns. His mother was explaining why they would soon be leaving New York for London, where the boy had never been. He did not take her seriousness seriously when she told him of the new home and the new school which he would find on the other side of the Atlantic. He could not imagine that they would ever leave a place in which, whenever he thought about it later, he imagined that he had always been happy.

His mother broke off from giving him the news which she was sure hurt her more than it hurt him, and pointed upwards. A silvered lozenge, slim and unearthly, seemed to be drifting soundlessly northwards on some celestial tide in the direction of Long Island. The boy pretended to marvel at what interrupted his wish not to think of the new life which threatened him.

They walked past the Spanish and Portuguese synagogue, with its sentinel pillars and its serried railings to which one day the previous winter he had clung: to avoid being hurled across the street in the knifing wind that roared up from Columbus Circle. He enjoyed his fear, like some new flavour. When he reached the apartment, he had frostbite under his chin. His mother's attention gave a dividend to the numb pain. Everything that went wrong in those first seven years of his life seemed to add to their charm.

They turned down West 70th Street and went under the steel-braced awning of their apartment house. Sam the janitor saluted the mother and prodded a finger into the boy's middle, as if he saw some invisible elevator button right there. Upstairs, as soon as Michael's mother had put down her packages, she turned on the radio. It had a fretwork fan over the brown mesh of the loudspeaker. A commentator was describing the arrival of the great airship whose silver needle had stitched the earlier sky. His mother's I Miller heels made

19

smart sounds as she went from hall to kitchen and back. Then they stopped. She called to the boy, who was building a skyscraper with wooden blocks in his room. 'Come and listen to this,' she said. 'This is terrible.'

The boy sighed, and whispered 'Nuts', and she had to call him again: 'Michael, quickly, you'll never forget this.' He knocked over his Empire State Building and went to the living-room door. His mother was tearful. It made him cold.

'You've almost missed it,' she said.

'*What?*'

She could only point to the voice on the radio. It spoke of flames and then degenerated into sobs. The emotion seemed like a show. The boy shifted his feet and wished that the terrible thing had not happened.

'It crashed,' his mother said. 'The zeppelin. It was just landing and then it . . . it burst into flames. Think of all those poor people.'

He tried, but the phrase 'poor people' reminded him less of the unseen victims of the Hindenburg disaster than of the poor people whom they had passed, when driving home in the Dodge back from a visit to Chicago, lining up for soup. Who were these silent, drab men in their cabs and collarless shirts? 'Poor people,' his father said, in his Oxford accent, 'who haven't got jobs.' The line was very long.

'You've got a job, Daddy, haven't you?'

'Thank God,' his father said.

Now his father's job was taking them to England. The strength of the decision, taken at Head Office, was greater than that of the wind which had made the boy hold onto the winter railings of the synagogue. It was beyond appeal or question. His father had been promoted. They would spend a year or two in London and then they would come back to New York, in 1940 or 1941, and his father would have an office very possibly with more than one telephone. It would be selfish to complain, wouldn't it, when Daddy would have more money and more opportunity if they went to England? He would get to know his father's country and his family, whom he had never seen. The boy said, 'You don't want to go either, do you, Mummy?' She said, 'Of course I do,' and gave him an angry kiss.

He did not believe the move would really happen. The next day he played as usual in Central Park. Red squirrels abounded in urgent stillness when he threw peanuts. They handed them to themselves with busy mouths. The Good Humour man came on his tricycle. Michael's mother bought ice-creams for him and for Elizabeth Jane, who always played with him and Jimmy Heller. The ice-creams were on sticks. If you were very lucky, as you licked the smooth yellow stick clean you discovered the words 'Good Humour' on it, which entitled you to a free one next time. Michael was torn between the urge to make his ice-cream last and the ambition to find that he had another one coming to him.

When their belongings were packed, the clothes went into cabin trunks much taller than the boy. He could almost have lived in one of them, with its hanging space and its big drawers and its brass hinges and its snappy pair of locks. One of the trunks was labelled NOT WANTED ON VOYAGE. It would be in the hold on the way across, his mother explained. They would see it again later. 'Like New York,' the boy said.

People came to the SS *Georgic* to see them off. The Scheuers came, and the Lehmanns, the Wallaces and the Goodmans, but Elizabeth Jane was at school, wasn't she? The stateroom was exciting with flowers and cellophaned fruit and bottles with nice messages on them. Michael watched his mother for proof that she knew that something terrible was happening, but her tears were all laughter.

They stayed in a service flat on the Cromwell Road until they found a permanent place. Michael went to the Science Museum, where he pressed buttons and interestings things were supposed to happen. He was introduced to his new family of antique aunts whose husbands were more often at their offices or on the golf course or dead than in the brown mansion flats where their wives or widows rang for trolleyed tea. His aunts, who were all great-aunts, impressed upon Michael that he must flatten his 'a's' and abandon all nostalgia for America, a country which, if his mother did not mind them saying so, was lacking in culture. Michael drew as little of London into his spiritual lungs as he could manage. Soon, he believed he would be taking deep breaths of reality again. One day, though, he took off his cap to Queen Mary.

That September morning, they were staying in a country house belonging to one of his father's Oxford friends. Michael was called from playing with the electric car belonging to the fat son of the house in order to listen to an old man talking on the wireless. The adults had taken the portable radio under the chestnut tree where they were having coffee. Michael listened to the foreign voice, chesty with emotions the boy did not understand, and he heard that evil things were going to be fought. Michael looked at his father, whose lower lip was sticking out, and wondered when he would be promoted back to America.

Michael was sent away to school. When he cried, he was told that he would have to be a brave soldier. It seemed to him that soldiers had a much better time than he did. They were shown on newsreels, waving and giving the thumbs-up on their way to France to hang up their washing. At boarding school, the main lesson was deceit. He paraded his new accent as others did their gasmasks, protection against being caught out. The present was a trap from which he might, one day, escape to be again what no one must guess he was or had ever been.

Many years later he read about a man who had died and had been discovered, at the post mortem, to have been twins. The atrophied other person he might also have been was crushed inside him, like some forgotten costume in an old trunk. It had eventually strangled him from within, choking his vital organs with its sullen invasion. Michael's other self waited and mocked. It lived more in his head than in his body, which grew with orange juice, and halibut liver oil and Radio Malt and dried eggs and all the things little boys were made of while millions died and were murdered and commentators became unsurprised when they spoke of the unspeakable.

His cousin Milton in the American Air Force was shot after

he had been captured near Arnhem. Michael's mother wore his pilot's wings, which made the boy wish that he too had been killed, if only he could be alive afterwards to enjoy his mother's proud grief.

The boy was no longer a child when the war ended. The cheering crowds and the hatted statesmen announced a victory which made Michael more anxious than thrilled. They spoke of the world going forward, but he wanted it to go back. When he saw the bulldozers tidying the soft bodies of Europe, his father wept and tried to say why. Michael said, 'Poor people.' His English accent said the right things, but the raucous, unscarred twin inside him cheered that all the obstacles were now removed. America could be home again.

He had won a scholarship to a school he had never heard of before the crested papers were thrust in front of him. He answered with indifferent fluency. He was trained to compete for a prize he never wanted. When he won it, his father said that it would be unfair to deny him the opportunity to be an English gentleman.

The boy went to queue for Picasso with his still young mother, who still wore the black-and-white tailored suit from Bonwit Teller which had come with them in the cabin trunk he had seen in their cellar, labelled NOT WANTED ON VOYAGE, when he went to dump toys he no longer played with. At the 93 and 85 bus stop, his mother said, 'Don't worry, you're not the only reason we're staying in England.' She had kept the American vowels he had lost. She was an unspoilt woman and was wearing the same I Miller shoes she had worn when the Hindenburg crashed and no one gloated at the German flames.

He went away to the school where he had won his scholarship. He suffered its privileged barbarities and cold comforts. Striped like any other humbug, he mouthed hymns and pretended to pray to King James's God. He marched in step and sloped arms and was congratulated on his keenness by inspecting officers. Only his tongue, for all its British bray, was sometimes rough with alien sarcasm. It made him no friends.

A few years later, his American grandfather had a serious heart attack. In his last summer before he was due to take the Cambridge scholarship exam, Michael and his mother sailed in the MV *Britannic* for New York. Michael's father had to work, although his career had been blighted by his refusal to return to the States. On the boat, as they bet on wooden horses, the boy's mother told him that his demanding (and now widowed) English grandmother had determined his father to stay in London.

There had been a victory but no war in New York. No weeds grew on bomb-sites, nothing was in short supply. Michael's school uniform, with its fly-buttoned hairiness, was a hot embarrassment in the summer heat. The Scheuers and the Lehmanns and the Wallaces and the Walkers were prompt with hospitality. They had not changed. Jimmy Heller now drove a car. Elizabeth Jane was pretty and had breasts.

He took her to the movies. He dared to hold her hand during *The Invisible Man* and put his lips against her hair during *The Scoundrel* while wicked things were said by Noël Coward. The girl smiled at them and then at him and the way she turned her face to him was an invitation he answered more promptly than he would have dared in London. Her lips reminded him of Good Humour, the strawberry flavour, and the hope of further, hidden treats.

They walked across Central Park, after playing midnight ping-pong in a basement arcade on Times Square. She assumed that he had already done all the things he was doing for the first time. She was the nice school he had never attended. The next time they met, she wore an off-the-shoulder blouse. Because it was hot, she said. New York weather made possible what was inconceivable in buttoned London. How could he, with her breast in his hand, ever care again about the Greek optative? He would, he told his mother, like to stay in New York for ever. Why had she seemed so angry at his saying what she must be feeling?

On their last night before the *Queen Mary* sailed, he took the girl to the theatre. In the interval, a man in a dinner jacket said to him, as he was taking drinks to the girl, 'Now hear this! I'll bet you're one hell of a ladies' man!' On the couch afterwards, he made the girl promise she would write if he wrote. She smiled and said, 'Just try me!' The next morning, when they met for early last kisses, she went with him to a department store where he bought a pair of fawn pants, with a zipper on them, just like the ones which American officers had worn.

When he returned to school, he packed the fawn trousers, which fitted almost too well. He put them on before he went up to Cambridge to take the scholarship, although he wanted to go to Oxford. Ashworth said, 'What have we here?'

'Independence Day,' Michael said.

'Yankee-doodle-dandy, eh?'

'Damn right,' he said. 'It's a little late this year.'

Cambridge was compensation, of a kind, for the letter, on scented paper, which told him that Elizabeth Jane was going to marry Jimmy Heller in the spring. His inner twin murmured, 'Now hear this: be a ladies' man,' while his upper lip aped British stiffness.

MAN IN A FLIGHT-BAG

Greg Snow

Greg Snow has written plays and stories for BBC Radio. His first novel, *Surface Tension*, was published last year. He is now working on a second and also on a stage-play. He lives in London.

'Man in a Flight-Bag' was first broadcast on Radio 4, read by Stephen Tompkinson.

It had all been started by the razor-blade. Freddy couldn't have known it then, but he knows now. He couldn't have known that something so simple as a razor-blade would lead him to his present unhappy position. He stares miserably at the blue vinyl walls of his prison as the dim light filters through the zip in the ceiling. For the hundredth time he curses the morning when Wayne Spendlove returned from Japan.

Wayne Spendlove cultivated a variety of swaggers. His general-purpose swagger, which he called walking, was only mildly irritating. Its arrogance was forgivable, buckish; like that of a young chimpanzee. Freddy had once left a banana on Wayne's desk, each day for a week. Wayne had merely eaten them. His second swagger, reserved for the company of attractive women, was definitely irritating. Freddy wondered how Wayne managed to walk at all with his pelvis at ninety degrees to his spine. He did, though, and an irking number of attractive women seemed content to walk alongside him.

On the morning of Wayne's return from Japan he bowled into the office using swagger Number Three. This Freddy found so annoying that he lit a cigarette, despite already having one smouldering in his ashtray. It was an obscene swagger: the same chimpanzee, but after a body-building course and a big win on the Pools. The worst thing was that people actually *liked* Wayne. The other men in the office went laddie in his presence. They grabbed at the secretaries' bottoms and frequently exposed their own. At lunch they drank too much, then shouted 'Go for it!' every other sentence.

So, Wayne had returned from his sales trip to Japan. He might have been an entire football team, such was his reception. After struggling through his fans (why don't they just *carry* him, Freddy wondered?) he opened his flight-bag. The lads gathered round his desk, expectant. What would it be this time? The latest electronic gadget? Or some more of that particularly frank Japanese pornography? It turned out to be neither. Nobody could work it out – it looked like a tiny, aluminium Hammerhead shark; or a high-tech auctioneer's gavel. Wayne was smug.

'No, Dal. S'not an ice-pick,' he said to unimaginative Darren. And 'No, Tel. S'definitely not one of *them*,' to the more imaginative Terry. 'D'ya give up?' he smirked. 'Awright, I'll tell ya.'

'No! Don't tell me. It's a . . .' They all stared at Freddy, who had risen from his chair and now walked, transfixed, towards Wayne.

'Well?' said Wayne.

'It's an integrated razor-blade and shaving-foam,' blurted Freddy.

Wayne wore the look of the freshly-robbed. Freddy watched him trying to invent something else the object could be, but it was hopeless.

'S'right,' he pouted. 'How d'you know?'

'I've no idea,' said Freddy. 'It just came to me.'

The others seemed to resent Freddy almost as much as Wayne did. They shuffled off to their desks, their ritual in ruins. When Wayne swaggered over he'd reverted to Number One. Sarcastically he pointed out that Freddy was smoking two cigarettes at once. But Freddy could not have cared. It was an important moment in his life.

He was lost after that. Something, some switch in his head, had been pulled. The idea of saving space in his *own* flight-bag became an obsession. He'd played at it before, but never seriously. He had a Pac-A-Mac, and one of those curly things which lets you make a cup of tea anywhere in the world (provided you're within two feet of an electric socket). But the idea had never really excited him as it did now. His first *affaire* was with a travel iron. It was a lovely little thing, all pink and white. It nestled in his hand; so graceful, so light, so space-saving. He had to admit that it wasn't much use as an iron, but that was beside the point. The way it slipped into one corner of his flight-bag, like a model into a couture gown, gave Freddy a unique thrill. Hours were spent in his bedroom, just pulling it out and putting it in again.

The thrill diminished, of course. Soon Freddy was in search of new pleasures. Whilst his friends contented themselves with matt-black midi systems or matt-black German hatchbacks, Freddy slaked his consumer-lust on the miniature. Some folding hangers gave him a cheap thrill. A butane-powered hairdrier satisfied him, for a whole fortnight. But gadgets soon lost their sexiness. Freddy needed fresh blood.

It might have been South Molton Street, or Covent Garden. Freddy couldn't remember anything but the hot wave of excitement crashing over him when he'd discovered the clothes. They were not attractive – shapeless and all the same bilious shade of green. They were not practical – the label said: NOT TO BE WASHED. AVOID HUMID CLIMATES. They certainly weren't cheap – the trousers alone cost £90. But they *were* – what? Collapsible? Shrinkable? The thing was, they could be crammed into a matchbox. He stood outside the shop for five minutes, gazing at the clothes. They were arranged half in their matchboxes and half spilling out. It was outrageous. He wanted them so badly he could feel them through the glass. His credit card took on a life of its own and appeared unbidden in his hand. Ten seconds later he stood shaking at the counter.

'Yes, sir?' she said. It was a she. A young one.

'The clothes. The green clothes in the window.'

'Brill, aren't they?' she smiled. 'Japanese.'

'Would you?' God, Japanese. Freddy's left knee was going like a sewing machine. He was dying.

While she was gone Freddy wiped the sweat from his credit card. In a second it was wet again, so he clamped it between his teeth and hoped he didn't drool.

He'd had a bath. He'd talcum-powdered himself into a coughing fit. He'd double-locked the front door. The moment was upon him. The collapsible clothes came in customised caskets, like coffins for shrews. Freddy spent a little time – an hour, perhaps, opening and closing the boxes. He wondered whether he could postpone the real pleasure until the next day, but he knew it was useless to try. He had to see how they fitted into his flight-bag.

Afterwards, limp with satisfaction, he performed his nightly ritual with the bathroom scales. His flight-bag still weighed less than ten pounds even though it contained enough accessories to set up home. Freddy went to bed happier than he had been for weeks.

The annual sales conference loomed. In the past, Freddy had dreaded five days in Düsseldorf with the massed reps of International Snap-Fit Plastics. This one, his fourth, would be different. Elvis Jones and Wayne Spendlove were to be his roommates. It had happened before. Two years previously he had suffered nightly the indignity of watching Wayne return to their room with multiple women. Once, Wayne had tossed a woman his way, as though he were Henry the Eighth and she a chewed chicken-leg. Freddy had walked with her along Birkenstrasse and discussed Goethe – it had seemed the decent thing to do. But he'd known that the woman, despite her humiliation, still wished she were with Wayne. What was it with louts and lasses, with boors and girls?

This year he would have a weapon. Even if Wayne-pasha installed a harem, even if his sales figures were positively numinous, nothing could dim the power of Freddy's flight-bag. As conference-time drew nearer, so did Freddy's self-assurance grow. Over and over he imagined that first glorious evening in the hotel room. There they would be – Wayne, Elvis and he. Elvis would be complaining that the mini-bar contained no *English* lager. Wayne would be laying out his panoply of see-thru underwear, commenting upon their erotic potential. Then he, Freddy, would begin unpacking The Flight-Bag. He knew the order it would take. First the more mundane items: the foldaway toothbrush and concentrated toothpaste; the nylon clothes-line with its Lilliputian clothes-pegs. Then he would up the ante with the folding iron and the butane hairdrier. And *then* he would bayonet Wayne's ego with the collapsible clothes. Even in rehearsal, Freddy could scarcely keep from screaming with triumph.

The morning of the flight to Düsseldorf and something is wrong. No, not *wrong*; just not quite right. Freddy has packed and repacked the bag a dozen times, with a growing feeling of futility. Time is getting short – nine o'clock, and the flight at midday. What is it? Not the arrangement of items in the bag: that is perfect, everything placed for maximum dramatic effect when the moment comes. And not the items themselves – he knows Wayne's envy will be crippling. Then he realises. Him. He is the problem. What glory is there in having the world's most perfectly compact collection of flight-bag accessories when he remains this ugly, oversized, *unminiature* lump of humanity?

There is space in the bag. Lots of it. Freddy shoves in his head and shoulders with no trouble at all. It seems natural for the rest of him to follow. With a chuckle he does up the zip, then turns to make himself more comfortable. This will force Wayne Spendlove to walk erect for evermore. Still chuckling at his own cleverness Freddy goes to undo the zip when he hears the noise of his front door being opened. He's forgotten the imminent arrival of Mrs Humfreys, his cleaning lady. Knowing (from her own interminable accounts) that her heart is her chief source of anguish, he doesn't wish to leap from the bag and cause her collapse. So he sits tight. He hears her in the kitchen and curses himself for not seizing the moment to escape. After that it is too late. She bangs into his bedroom carrying the wireless, which blares Radio 2 at stentorian volume.

'Wiv a little bit o' luck, wiv a little bit o' luck, wiv a little bit o' bloomin' LUCK!' caw Mrs Humfreys and Stanley Holloway, indivisibly. He hears her puffing, complaining about the weight of something she was trying to move. Then the something, whatever it is, crushes the flight-bag and Freddy inside it. When he recovers his wind he yells at the top of his lungs to an indifferent Mrs Humfreys.

'Stayand bah yore mayan! Give hyam two arms to clang to . . .' Mrs Humfreys and Tammy Wynette duet. The slam of the bedroom door seals Freddy's fate. Bitterly he realises he had never thought to buy any miniature food.

'Wonder where Freddy's got to?' asks Elvis Jones casually, looking at his watch.

'Search me,' says Wayne Spendlove, swaggering across the departure lounge to a coffee-machine. 'Who cares? Bleeding yuppy.'

'Yeah,' agrees Elvis. 'Bleeding yuppy.'

''Ere,' says Wayne. 'Wanna sneak preview of my new knicker collection?'

'Yeah,' Elvis leers. 'Go for it.'

BLUE POPPIES

Jane Gardam

Jane Gardam was born in North Yorkshire and now lives in East Kent. She has published numerous novels for children and adults and is a prolific short-story writer. *God on the Rocks* was a runner-up for the Booker Prize in 1978. Most recently she has written *The Queen of the Tambourine*, which won the 1991 Whitbread Award for the best novel.

'Blue Poppies' was first broadcast on Radio 4, read by Anna Massey.

My mother died with her hand in the hand of the Duchess. We were at Clere in late summer. It was a Monday. Clere opens on Mondays and Tuesdays only. It is not a great house and the Duke likes silence. It offers only itself. 'No teas, no toilets!' I once heard a woman on one of the very few coaches that ever found its way there say. 'It's not much, is it?' Clere stands blotchy and moulding and its doves look very white against its peeling portico. Grass in the cobbles. If you listen hard you can hear a stable clock still thinly strike the quarters.

Mother had been staying with me for a month, sometimes knowing me, sometimes looking interestedly in my direction as if she ought to. Paddling here, paddling there. Looking out of windows, saying brightly, 'Bored? Of course I'm not bored.' Once or twice when I took her breakfast in bed she thought I was a nurse. Once after tea she asked if she could play in the garden and then looked frightened. Today was showery. She watched the rain and the clouds blowing.

'Would you like to go to Clere?'

'Now what is that?'

'You know. You've been before. It's the place with the blue poppies.'

'Blue poppies?'

'You saw them last time.'

'*Meconopsi?*' she said. 'I really ought to write letters.'

My mother was ninety-one and she wrote letters every day. She had done so since she was a girl. She wrote at last to a very short list of people. Her address book looked like a tycoon's diary. Negotiations completed. Pages crossed off. The more recent crossings-off were wavery.

We set off for the blue poppies and she wore a hat and gloves and surveyed the rainy world through the car window. Every now and then she opened her handbag to look at her pills or wondered aloud where her walking-stick had gone.

'Back seat.'

37

'No,' she said. 'I like the front seat in a car. It was always manners to offer the front seat. It's the best seat, the front seat.'

'But the stick is on the back seat.'

'What stick is that?'

At Clere the rain had stopped, leaving the grass slippery and a silvery dampness hanging in the air. The Duchess was on the door, taking tickets. That is to say she was behind a rickety trestle-table and working in a border nearby. She was digging. On the table a black tin box stood open for small change and a few spotted postcards of the house were arranged beside some very poor specimens of plants for sale at exorbitant prices. The Duchess's corduroy behind rose beyond them. She straightened up and half turned to us, great gloved hands swinging, caked in earth.

The Duchess is no beauty. A beak of ivory and deep-sunken hard blue eyes. Her hair is scant and colourless. There are ropes in her throat. Her face is weather-beaten and her haunches strong for she has created the gardens at Clere almost alone. When she speaks, the voice of the razorbill is heard in the land.

The Duke. Oh, the poor Duke! We could see him under the portico seated alone at another rough table, eating bread. There was a slab of processed cheese beside the bread and a small bottle of beer. He wore a shawl and his face was long and rueful. His nearside shoulder was raised at a defensive angle to the Duchess, as if to ward off blows. I saw the Duchess see me pity the neglected Duke as she said to us, 'Could you hold on? Just a moment?' and turning back to the flower-bed began to heave at a great, leaden root. My mother opened her bag and began to scrabble in it.

'Now, this is my treat.'

'There!' cried the Duchess, heaving the root aloft, shaking off soil, tossing it down. 'Two, is it?'

'*Choisya ternata*,' said my mother. 'One and a half.'

A pause.

'For the house, is it? Are you going round the house as well as the garden?'

'We really came just for the poppies,' I said, 'and it's two, please.'

'Oh, I should like to see the house,' said my mother. 'I saw the poppies when I stayed with Lilian last year.'

I blinked.

'Lilian thinks I can't remember,' my mother said to the Duchess. 'This time I should like to see the house. And I shall pay.'

'Two,' I signalled to the Duchess, smiling what I hoped would be a collaborative smile above my mother's head. I saw the Duchess think, 'A bully.'

'One and a half,' said my mother.

'Mother, I am over fifty. It is children who are half-price.'

'And Senior Citizens,' said my mother. 'And I am one of those, as I'm sure Her Grace will believe. I can prove it if I can only find my card.'

'I'll trust you,' said the Duchess. Her eyes gleamed on my mother. Then her icicle-wax face cracked into a smile, drawing the thin skin taut over her nose. 'I'm a Lilian, too,' she said and gave a little cackle that told me she thought me fortunate.

We walked about the ground floor of the house, though many corridors were barred, and small ivory labels hung on hooks on many doors. They said PRIVATE in beautifully painted copperplate. In the drawing room where my mother felt a little dizzy – nothing to speak of – there was nowhere to sit down. All the sofas and chairs were roped off, even the ones with torn silk, or stuffing sprouting out. We were the only visitors and there seemed to be nobody in attendance to see that we didn't steal the ornaments. 'Meissen I'd think, dear,' said my mother, picking up a little enamel box from a table. 'Darling, oughtn't we to get this valued?' On other tables stood photographs in silver frames. On walls hung portraits in carved and gilded frames. Here and there across the centuries shone out the Duchess's nose.

'Such a disadvantage,' said my mother. 'Poor dear. That

photograph is a Lenare. He's made her very hazy. That was his secret, you know. The haze. He could make anybody look romantic. All the fat young lilies. It will be her engagement portrait.'

'I'm surprised her mother let her have it done.'

'Oh, she would have had to. It was very much the thing. Like getting confirmed. Well, more usual really than getting confirmed with these people. She looks as though she'd have had no truck with it. I agree. I think she seems a splendid woman, don't you?'

We walked out side by side and stood on the semicircular marble floor of the porch, among the flaking columns. The Duke had gone. The small brown beer bottle was on its side. Robins were pecking about among the crumbs of bread. The Duchess could be seen, still toiling in the shrubs. Mother watched her as I considered the wet and broken steps down from the portico and up again towards the gardens, and my fury at my mother's pleasure in the Duchess. I wondered if we might take the steps one by one, arm in arm, with the stick and a prayer.

'Who is that person over there?' asked Mother. 'Digging in that flower-bed? A gardener I suppose. They often get women now. I should like to have done that.'

Down and up the steps we went and over the swell of the grass slope. There was a flint arch into a rose-garden and a long white seat under a *gloire de Dijon* rose. 'I think I'll sit,' said my mother.

'The seat's wet.'

'Never mind.'

'It's sopping.'

She sat and the wind blew and the rose shook drops and petals on her. 'I'll just put up my umbrella.'

'You haven't an umbrella.'

'Don't be silly, dear, I have a beautiful umbrella. It was Margaret's. I've had it for years. It's in the hall-stand.'

'Well, I can't go all the way home for it.'

'It's not in your home, dear. You haven't got a hall-stand.

It's in *my* home. I'm glad to say I still have a home of my own.'

'Well I'm not going there,' I replied. 'It's a hundred miles. I'm not going a hundred miles for your umbrella.'

'But of course not. I didn't bring an umbrella to you, Lilian. Not on holiday. I told you when you collected me: "There's no need for me to bring an umbrella 'cause I can always use one of yours." Lilian, this seat is very wet.'

'For heaven's sake then — Come with me to see the blue poppies.'

The Duchess's face suddenly peered round the flint arch and disappeared again.

'Lilian, such a very strange woman just looked into this garden. Like a hawk.'

'Mother, I'm going to see the poppies. Are you coming?'

'I saw them once before. I'm sure I did. They're very nice, but I think I'll just sit.'

'Nice!'

'Yes, *nice* dear. *Nice.* You know I can't enthuse like you can. I'm not very imaginative. I never have been.'

'That is true.'

'They always remind me of Cadbury's chocolates, but I can never remember why.'

I thought, senile. I must have said it.

'Well, yes. I dare say I am. Who is this woman approaching with a cushion? How very kind. Yes, I would like a cushion. My daughter forgot the umbrella. How thoughtful. She's clever, you see. She went to a university. Very clever, and imaginative, too. She insisted on coming all this way — such a wet day and of course most of your garden is over — because of the blue of the poppies. Children are so funny, aren't they?'

'I never quite see why everybody gets so worked up about the blue,' said the Duchess.

'*Meconopsis baileyi*,' said my mother.

'Yes.'

'*Betonicifolia.*'

'Give me *Campanula carpatica*,' said the Duchess.

'Ah! Or *Gentiana verna "Angulosa"*,' said my mother. 'We sound as if we're saying our prayers.'

The two of them looked up at me. My mother regarded me with kindly attention, as if I were a pleasant acquaintance she would like to think well of. 'You go off,' said the Duchess. 'I'll stay here. Take your time.'

As I went I heard my mother say, 'She's just like her father, of course. You have to understand her. She hasn't much time for old people. And of course, she's no gardener.'

When I came back – and they were: they were just like Cadbury's chocolate papers crumpled up under the tall black trees in a sweep, the exact colour, lying about among their pale hairy leaves in the muddy earth, raindrops scattering them with a papery noise – as I came back, the Duchess was holding my mother's hand and looking closely at her face.

She said, 'Quick. You must telephone. In the study. Left of the portico. Says Private on a disc. Run.' She let go the hand that fell loose. Loose and finished. The Duchess seemed to be smiling. A smile that stretched the narrow face and stretched the lines sharper round her eyes. It was more a sneer than a smile. I saw she was sneering with pain. I said, 'My mother is dead.' She said, 'Quick. Run. Be quick.'

I ran, ran down the slope, over the porch to the study, where the telephone was old and black and lumpen and the dial flopped and rattled. All done, I ran out again and stood at the top of the steps looking up the grassy slope. We were clamped in time. Round the corner of the house came the Duke in a wheelchair pushed by a woman in a dark blue dress. She had bottle legs. They looked at me with suspicion. The Duke said, 'Phyllis,' to the woman and continued to stare.

'Yes?' asked the woman. 'Yes? What is it? Do you want something?' I thought, 'This last day again.'

I walked up the slope to the rose-garden where the Duchess sat looking over the view. She said, 'Now she has died.' She seemed to be grieving. I knew though that my mother had not been dead when I ran for the telephone and if it had been the Duchess who had run for the telephone I should have

42

been with my mother when she died. So then I hated the Duchess and all her works.

And it was two years later that I came face to face with her again, at a luncheon party given in aid of the preservation of trees, and quite the other side of the country. There were the usual people – some eccentrics, some gushers, some hard-grained, valiant fund-raisers. No village people. The rich. All elderly. All, even the younger ones, belonging to what my children call 'the old world'. They had something of the ways of my mother's generation but none of them was my mother.

The Duchess was over in a corner, standing by herself and eating hugely, her plate up near her mouth, her fork, working away, her eyes swivelling frostily about. She saw me at once and went on staring as she ate. I knew she meant that I should go across to her.

I had written a letter of thanks, of course, and she had not only replied adequately – an old thick cream card inside a thick cream envelope and an undecipherable signature – but she had sent flowers to the funeral.

That had ended it.

I watched with interest as the Duchess cut herself a good half-pound of cheese and put it in her pocket. Going to a side-table she opened her handbag and began to sweep fruit into it. Three apples and two bananas disappeared, and people around her looked away. As she reached the door she looked across at me. She did not exactly hesitate but there was something. Then she left the house.

But in the car-park, there she was in a filthy car, eating one of the bananas. Still staring ahead, she wound down a window and I went towards her.

She said, 'Perhaps I ought to have told you. Your mother said to me, "Goodbye Lilian dear".'

'Your name is Lilian,' I said. 'She was quite capable of calling *you* Lilian. She had taken a liking to you. Which she never did to me.'

'No, no. She meant you,' said the Duchess. 'She said, "I'm sorry, darling, not to have gone with you to the poppies."'

BLOW-PIPE

Michael Carson

Michael Carson was born in Merseyside and has worked in various countries including Saudia Arabia, Brunei and Iran. He has contributed over twenty stories to BBC Radio and has published four novels. He is now working on number five and continues to write for *Short Story* on Radio 4.

'Blow-Pipe' was first broadcast on Radio 4, read by Anna Massey.

From *The Little Bentley Sentinel*, 4 March 1948

It is with great regret that we announce the death of Mr Cecil Puckeridge who passed away on Sunday last while tolling the great bell at St Cuthbert's. Mr Puckeridge – Cess to his many friends in the village – will long be remembered for his support of the Little Bentley Hunt, and his sterling work on behalf of the Territorial Army. He is survived by his unmarried daughter, Agatha.

The Little Bentley Sentinel, 10 January 1949

It was half past ten when we all gathered at Little Bentley railway station to bid farewell to Miss Agatha Puckeridge at the start of her journey to Borneo, where she will be working as a lay missionary to spread the Light of Truth among the wild people of that benighted island.

The vicar of St Cuthbert's told her that she would be in our prayers. I am sure all readers of *The Sentinel* will devoutly second that motion.

Good luck, Agatha Puckeridge! God speed!

The Little Bentley Sentinel, 12 May 1949

Dear Editor:
I am writing to you because I am sure your readers would like to hear some news regarding dear Agatha Puckeridge and her progress with the missions in Borneo. This week a letter arrived.

After a tiresome sea voyage, Agatha landed at the town of Kuching on the west coast of Borneo. Agatha was charmed by this town which has a very large population of cats. She tells me that 'Kuching' actually means 'cat' in the local language. At Kuching, Agatha rested a few days and then embarked on a smaller ship for Kuala Baram, three hundred miles north-east along the coast, from whence she was taken by river steamer up the Baram River to Marudi.

It is from Marudi that she wrote the letter. There she is learning the language of the Penan tribe, naked jungle-dwellers who inhabit the area upriver from Marudi. I detected in her letter a certain trepidation at finding herself so far from home. At first, she says, she was afraid to go out onto the streets because of the near-naked men and their bare-breasted wives. It seemed such a long way from Little Bentley, she said. One interesting fact she mentions is that in Marudi the natives employ long hollow wooden tubes and blow darts from the end. One morning she saw a man blow one of these darts into a dog. The dog stumbled along for a moment and then dropped dead! Agatha said she was shocked at the sight, but knew she would have to come to terms with such barbarity, while hoping that she would be able to wean the people from this and other – unmentionable – barbaric practices.

Agatha asks for your prayers as she embarks on the final stage of her journey.

Madge Elmstead

The Sentinel, 30 November 1949

Dear Mr Tendring:
I was very pleased to receive the copy of *The Sentinel* in which you had included the letter of dear Madge Elmstead. I was also delighted that you should request a periodic letter from Borneo.

I have now been at the mission station of Mulu for a month. I am writing this during a fierce rainstorm. The heavy drops of rain plop on to my leaf roof. Some children and a dog have come to my little hut for shelter. The mission consists solely of myself, I'm afraid. Without the visits from the children I should be very lonely indeed.

I fear that so far I have not made any converts. Mulu is situated near the confluence of two rivers, the Baram and the Nagas. We are on the Baram, just a few hundred yards upstream from the place where the two rivers meet. Around the corner, on the bank of the Nagas, is a Catholic mission which has been here much longer than we have. I'm sorry to say that most of the Penan have already been swallowed up by the rapacious jaws of Popery. You see, the Catholic fathers came armed with rosaries, medals and holy pictures, while I have just five copies of the Book of Common Prayer. The people are simple. It is hard to tell them the obvious advantages of Anglicanism over the Roman Church. They at once fall in love with the baubles – all the things that we at St Cuthbert's so frown upon.

Last week I met the blow-pipe maker. He lives upriver from the mission. Reading Madge's letter to you I see that she mentioned the incident in Marudi when a tribesman killed a dog with one of these contraptions. Watching the blow-pipe maker, whose name is Cantab, is an education. He is very amiable and a widower. He has not so far given way to Rome, and I have high hopes that he will be my first convert. Cantab makes the most wonderful blow-pipes with the crudest tools imaginable. When he has finished, one can look through the nine-foot hole and see a perfect circle of daylight at the other end.

A blow-pipe is very easy to use. One takes a needle-thin sliver of wood about nine inches in length and dips it into a poison. At one end of the dart, there is a round, spongy flight which fits snugly into the hole of the blow-pipe. Then one aims the blow-pipe towards the quarry and blows hard. The dart flies out of the other end, completely silent, completely invisible, and – with luck – kills the victim. It is then possible to retrieve the dart, and re-use it.

Cantab's skin is a beautiful burnt-wheat brown. He is as lightly muscled and as perfectly proportioned as a Greek god. What a fine catch he would be for the Anglican Church!

I plan to build a little school here. Also a clinic, though I fear my medical skills are rather rudimentary. If we cannot win souls, then we can at least provide some help for the dear bodies of these gentle but surprising people.

Agatha Puckeridge

The Sentinel, 31 March 1959

SALE OF WORK BREAKS ALL RECORDS

Last Saturday's Sale of Work in aid of the Cecil Puckeridge College in Mulu managed to collect £3,000. This is a one-third increase on the amount raised last year, and represents an all-time record.

As all you avid readers of Dame Agatha's monthly *Letter from Borneo* will be aware, the money will go straight into the college's Scout and Guide Uniforms Fund.

The Sentinel, 30 January 1969

LETTER FROM BORNEO
by Dame Agatha Puckeridge

It is really hard to credit that I have been in Borneo for twenty years. So very much and so very little has been achieved in that time. The two greatest triumphs are our college and dispensary and we have the people of Little Bentley and elsewhere to thank for all your generous support over the years. Ever since 1962, when the last Catholic missionaries were killed by the blow-pipes of unknown assailants, our efforts at conversion have borne fruit. I am happy to report that few of the tribal people still cling to their old beliefs. It all seems a very long time ago, when, led by Cantab – now of course our own dear Cuthbert – they joined the church in droves.

Several of you have written to me asking for news of Cuthbert, the blow-pipe maker. We are still fast friends and I am happy to report that he is in excellent health.

There is only one possible cloud on our horizon. The government keeps sending people to survey the forest and I worry that one day the loggers will arrive to attempt to tear down our Christian patch of Shangri-La. Cuthbert tells me not to worry, but I do ...

The Sentinel, 6 July 1981

FIGHTING ON GREEN DISRUPTS LITTLE BENTLEY–MULU SPONSORED HALF-MARATHON

Swarms of motor-bikes tore into Little Bentley on Saturday and disrupted the start of the sponsored half-marathon in aid of the Lady Alresford Agricultural College in Mulu, Borneo. The unruly youths from other villages upset the tea-stand, pulled down bunting and shouted abuse at the adjudicators. The police arrived, but not before an altercation had started between the ruffians and patrons of the Puckeridge Arms. Three arrests were made

The Sentinel, 9 March 1985

LETTER FROM BORNEO
by Dame Agatha Puckeridge

Well, after almost forty years in Borneo it seems that all is not as 'civilized' as I had thought. Regular readers of these little letters will know that we have been waging holy war on logging concerns for well over a decade now. It seems that every time the loggers made a foray into the environs of Mulu, a hitherto unknown group of Penans would attack them with their blow-pipes, the darts of which are spiked with a lethal poison. These periodic attacks had been sufficient to frighten away the loggers. However, as the whole of the lower Baram River becomes denuded of hardwood, the central government in Kuala Lumpur has been licking its lips when it sees our little Shangri-La on the map, still untouched. Cuthbert warned me that one day soldiers would be sent. I refused to believe it. Well, last month it happened. A group of troups landed by helicopter next to the hockey field and commenced terrorising anyone they could find. They pitched their tents on the hallowed turf of our cricket pitch and went off into the jungle looking for the tribes who had frightened away the loggers. They did not return and after a week Cuthbert and I went into the jungle to look for them. Alas, all had been killed by blow-pipe darts. The culprits had as usual melted away into the jungle.

The Sentinel, 1 August 1988

DAME AGATHA RETURNS TO LITTLE BENTLEY!

A throng of people turned out to welcome back to Little Bentley the woman who has put us on the map while she disappeared off it.

Asked about her reasons for her sudden return from Borneo, Dame Agatha said that it was really the death of Cuthbert, the blow-pipe maker, that had decided her to leave. The Cecil Puckeridge College, the St Cuthbert Dispensary, and the Lady Alresford Agricultural College in Mulu are all in safe hands.

Dame Agatha is to take up residence at Green View Cottage.

The Sentinel, 23 March 1989

CAN NO ONE STOP THESE VANDALS?

The spate of vandalism continues. Ten gravestones were found spray-painted with obscenities by the verger of St

Cuthbert's on Sunday morning last; the two telephone kiosks outside Green View Cottage have also been rendered unusable; Mr and Mrs Thorrington on their way back from Sunday service that same evening were abused by a group of youths. Mr Thorrington was also assaulted and is recovering in the Lady Wivenhoe Memorial Hospital.

The Sentinel, 10 April 1989

TWO BODIES FOUND IN LITTLE BENTLEY

Local residents of Little Bentley were shocked and horrified last Tuesday to discover the dead bodies of two youths during their early-morning walk. The bodies were lying in the cemetery of St Cuthbert's. One of the corpses was found to be in possession of a can of spray paint. Police sources told *The Sentinel* that forensic authorities have been unable to find any immediate cause for the deaths of the youths. However, the deaths bear an uncanny resemblance to the unexplained deaths of three youths in Colchester. They were struck down in the act of indecently assaulting a young girl outside a pub last month. Enquiries are continuing.

The Sentinel, 15 July 1989

DAME AGATHA SETTLING DOWN HAPPILY

After all the frightening news we have had to report recently it makes a pleasant change for your reporter to be able to visit our local celebrity, Dame Agatha Puckeridge. Doubly pleasant, because Dame Agatha was in fine form. We talked over tea in her comfy Laura Ashley sitting room. It was hard to imagine that this frail old lady had done such an amount of daring-do in her life. Next to the copper bed-warmer on the wall I saw what looked like a spear. It did not fit comfortably with the rest of the furnishings. I asked Dame Agatha about it. She looked up fondly at the object. 'That's my blow-pipe, my only souvenir of Mulu,' she said. 'Dear Cuthbert gave it to me on his death-bed. I keep it to remind me of him – and of all the good times we shared.'

'And are you settling down happily in Little Bentley after all those years away?' I asked her.

Dame Agatha smiled serenely. 'It has taken me a little time to settle back in. But you'd expect that, wouldn't you? Still, I feel I am carving out a little niche for myself here in Little Bentley. There are always things to do to make oneself useful – just as there were in Mulu – one simply has to look for them.' I left after tea, heartened and inspired by my visit to Dame Agatha Puckeridge. Truly it is consoling to know that an active little dynamo like Dame Agatha continues to lighten our darkness and lead us through these troubled times with her kindly light.

Long may she be a beacon to us!

WOMEN WAITING

Richard Nelson

Richard Nelson is one of America's leading drama-tists. His recent UK productions include *Some Americans Abroad* (RSC, Barbican) and *Two Shakespearean Actors* (RSC, Stratford), and he has now completed a new play, *Columbus and the Discovery of Japan*. He received a Time Out Award for *Principia Scriptoriae* (1987) and a Giles Cooper Award for his radio play *Languages Spoken Here* (1988).

'Women Waiting' was first broadcast on Radio 3, read by Shelley Thompson.

JAKE'S CABS is not an all-girl taxi company but it seems like one on Thursday nights. Helen, Taylor, and Frankie are three of JAKE'S eight part-time drivers, but by some fluke of scheduling on Thursdays they are the totality of JAKE'S public face. And an attractive face it is; black-haired Helen, looking nothing like the forty-one she claims, is perhaps the most beautiful, her skin the smoothest and best cared for, her colour the subtlest, her clothes the classiest. Taylor and Frankie, only twenty-one, dress like students which until two months ago they were, and both retain what clothes can never hide – the beauty of youth.

Three taxi-drivers would seem a little excessive for a village the size of Ralton, but in truth it isn't the village the taxis work but rather the Amtrak station which clings to a cliff on the edge of the Hudson River, and which three times an evening serves as the depository of numerous long-distance commuters, long-weekenders and locals home from a day in New York City, some ninety-nine miles to the south. Many of these travellers have come to rely upon JAKE'S as their best way to make the final connection to their country homes.

And every one of them on any Thursday this summer had the experience of first climbing down off the train and then back up the fifty or so stairs to the station, being greeted by the sight of three attractive women waiting, and by the words each woman would cry out: 'Taxi? Anyone need a taxi?'

'Train number 49, The Lake Shore Limited, to Hudson, Albany and All Points West is reported to be forty-five minutes late.' This from the loudspeaker located just above the taxi-stand.

'Forty-five minutes!' Taylor shakes her head in disgust and climbs onto the hood of Helen's cab, stretches out and rests her head on the windshield, much as she would on a lawn chair at the beach.

57

Frankie checks her watch. 'I might have a date tonight.'

Helen catches the eye of the stationmaster through his office window; he shrugs at her, helpless.

'Why don't we go and come back?' suggests Frankie. 'Just sitting here twiddling our thumbs, letting our lives pass before our –'

'Go where?' Taylor picks her head slowly off the windshield. 'Anywhere worth going we'd have to turn around and come back as soon as we got there.'

'Then maybe we don't come back.' Frankie stares at the ground. 'Let them find their own way home.'

'She has a date,' says Taylor.

'I don't,' says Helen, who has taken out a pack of cigarettes and has begun to light one. 'So I don't mind staying. Besides there's a nice breeze here.'

It has so far been a very hot and humid summer, setting all sorts of records.

'And even if I did have a date, not very likely being a forty-one-year-old divorcee with a twelve-year-old child, I still wouldn't let all of us leave. It just wouldn't be right. What if someone was stranded?' Helen holds up her hands. 'After all, don't forget what happened to that woman.'

'What woman?' Taylor nearly jumps off the windshield, she is sitting forward now. Frankie for the first time since the announced delay looks up.

'That's right, I keep forgetting you just started to drive for JAKE'S a few months ago.' Helen pulls at, then taps her cigarette. 'Still I'm amazed no one has told you.'

Behind their cabs, people in two other parked cars also wait to pick up their passengers. Their windows are open, to catch the breeze off the river.

'So tell us then. What happened?' Taylor slaps the hood lightly with her hand.

'It isn't a *short* story.' Helen looks towards Frankie.

'So? We aren't going anywhere, are we?' Taylor has turned to Frankie as well. 'Are we?'

'Then sit down and let her talk.'

Taylor slides over to what would be the driver's side, and

Frankie with some hesitation climbs onto the hood, sits herself upright and crosses her legs.

Helen, after patiently watching the girls settle, begins.

'Like tonight, the train was forty-five minutes late, and the taxi she had ordered to meet her had not waited.' Helen pauses to beat out her cigarette on the bottom of her running shoe.

'Of course this woman was furious, it was past eleven at night – the timetables have been changed since then – the last train was much later and the taxi station in the village was already closed. She tried to phone, of course, but only got the recording.'

One of the waiting cars has its motor turned on and drives off.

Helen continues: 'Her son and daughter were asleep, she assumed, so a call home for a ride at this time was not possible. She certainly did not want her sister, who was babysitting, to wake up the children, pack them into the car – they were too young to be left alone – just to drive the two miles from the village to the station to pick her up.' Helen turns to Frankie, 'You see what I mean about stranding people.'

'Maybe she had a date,' says Frankie. 'The driver, I mean.'

'What makes you think the driver was a woman? Perhaps there weren't any women drivers back then. Anyway, this lady has no other choice but to walk the two miles home, down a road without streetlights; the season was fall so the leaves were down and slippery, and these were hiding holes on the side of the road. One autumn I nearly broke an ankle falling into just such a boobytrap.'

'Does this end with her suing the taxi company?'

'Frankie, please, don't interrupt her.'

Pigeons can now be heard fluttering in the eves of the station.

'She has a suitcase,' Helen continues, taking out her last cigarette and lighting it. 'Not a very heavy one, but she has been away for three days and two nights.'

'Doing what?' asks Frankie. 'Business or pleasure?'

'I really don't know. Why don't we say a little of both.'

59

'Why don't we,' echoes Frankie, giving a look at Taylor.

'Wait a minute. Did this really happen or are we now making it up?' Taylor wants to know.

'You decide,' Helen says. 'So she'd started up the station steps into the parking lot, the suitcase sort of banging against each step. The other passengers from the train had long since driven off, while she had waited at the taxi stop and while she had called and received only the recording. Or rather she assumed they had all departed.' Helen puffs on the cigarette and turns towards the sound of the pigeons for a moment. 'So you can imagine her surprise, actually you could call it shock, when as she squeezed between two closely parked cars on her way towards the road, a voice called to her out of a shadow. "Need a lift?"'

'I see, it's a scary story. What, does he have a claw on one arm?' Taylor is interrupting now.

'How do you know it was a man's voice?' asks Helen, without even looking at Taylor. 'But of course it was.'

Helen pauses to let this revelation sink in. In the distance you can hear a rope banging in the wind, against the metal docking just across the tracks.

'He said more,' Helen continues. 'He said: "I heard you try the taxi company, but since I knew they'd be closed, I figured I'd better wait to see if you needed a lift. I am going past the village." She still hadn't seen his face, mind you; it was still in the shadow.'

'Wait, how did he know she was calling the taxi company? She just dialled, right?' Taylor looks towards Frankie. 'And then she only listened to the recording. She hadn't *said* anything.' Frankie turns to Helen.

'I don't know,' is all Helen can answer.

'And how did he know she was going into the village?' Frankie begins to question now. 'Did he know her?' Frankie's freckle face has now turned serious and concerned.

'I don't know,' answers Helen.

'Did she know him?' Taylor asks.

'No. But she got into his car, which was newish, comfortable, perhaps an import of some kind. Something small, certainly not a *family* car.'

'She just gets in? With no one around?' Taylor shakes her head. 'She deserved whatever she got.'

'Who says she got anything?' Helen smiles. 'What do you think is going to happen to her?'

'What did he look like?' interrupts Frankie. 'Are we talking about a young man or an old man?'

'How old is young?' asks Helen.

'Something around her own age.'

'Which is what? I haven't told you her age. She was thirty-two.' Helen drags on the cigarette. 'And he was a good deal older.'

'And no doubt very attractive,' adds Taylor.

'Make him interesting instead of attractive,' suggests Frankie, who turns to Taylor, 'so it'll be more realistic.'

'By the way,' Helen continues, 'when she got into the car, the passenger side was unlocked. I don't know what that means, but that's the one detail that makes my skin crawl.' She lets this thought, too, sink in on her audience before going on. 'He said nothing at first in the car, and she even had the impression, maybe even the fear, that he might say nothing for the whole ride.'

'She had to tell him where she lived,' Taylor turns to Frankie, 'didn't she?' Frankie doesn't move.

'But finally he does speak. He says: "I saw the book you were reading on the train."'

'He noticed her on the train!'

'Maybe she has it on her lap, Taylor,' Frankie adds with disgust.

'No,' Helen says, the arbiter of truth in this matter, 'the book was now safely tucked into her purse. He *had* noticed her on the train.'

'Oh,' is all Frankie can say, or rather gasp. A car comes down the road and passes the station, its lights sweeping over the three women.

Helen continues, 'She tried not to look at him as he spoke, but as he turned the steering-wheel clockwise at the point

where the road to the village turns, she could not help noticing the thick fingers with bushes of hair on the knuckles.'

'Great. I don't like hairy men,' Frankie adds.

'You're not the one in the car with him,' says Taylor.

Helen has picked up a maple twig off the parking lot and
has begun pulling at the leaves when they hear from the
speaker, 'Train 49, the northbound Lake Shore Limited, will
be arriving in five minutes.'

'Five minutes?' Frankie checks her watch.

'It must have picked up time at Croton. We should probably go in.'

'What about the woman? Finish telling what happened.'

'Actually,' Helen rips off a leaf from the twig, 'there's not
much more to tell.'

'There better be,' adds Frankie. 'This better not be a joke.
Remember there are times when each of us is out here alone.
So if this was just to try to scare me —'

'Okay. At the Inn she had a white wine.'

'The inn? What inn?' The girls stare at Helen.

'I'm trying to get to the end. Okay. She went to the Inn
with him.'

'Is that where he was staying?'

'No. His house was out of town. Many miles out of town.
He must have thought he couldn't ask her to go there.' Helen
says quite matter-of-factly, 'So she ended up at the Inn.
Though not immediately. She of course first refused his invitation and insisted on being taken home, which he did.'

'She let him see where she lived!'

'What else was she to do? Ask to be let off on some corner?'
Taylor says to Frankie.

'But as he was about to drive off, in fact, as he was driving
off, she ran back to the street and yelled to stop him. She had
changed her mind. She would have a drink. So she went
inside, came out again to say she was sorry, maybe another
time, but then her sister came out and insisted she was fine
staying and so she got back into the car and they parked in
the Inn lot and went in and she had a white wine.' The train

whistle could now be heard echoing across the river valley. 'We better go,' Helen says.

'Finish the story!' This was a threat now from both members of the audience.

'Well, he rented a room, they went upstairs, a few hours later they were both seen walking towards his car in the parking lot. And that,' Helen looks both young women in the eyes now, 'was the last time she was ever seen again.'

Helen turns and goes through the double doors and down the passage which leads to the platform stair. Frankie and Taylor are right behind her.

'The last time?' Taylor asks.

'Of course there were rumours,' Helen says as they walk. 'Three distinctly different ones. Around this time, an Arizona man was arrested further upstate for picking up female hitch-hikers and then suffocating them. The police showed him the woman's picture, but he said he couldn't remember if she had been "one of his" or not.'

'What about the house out of town?' asks Frankie. 'Why didn't they just check there?'

'I don't know. I suppose they did. If there was a house. I can only tell you what I've been told,' Helen replies, as they stand now on the top step of the platform, the train's headlights beginning to run along the tracks towards the station. 'Then there was the rumour that she had indeed run off with this man whom she hardly knew at all, married him, later sent for her children, and lived with him happily for years in Michigan or California. Though now they say he is dead. He was older, as I told you.'

The massive turbo engine is coming right at them now, the platform is flooded with light and noise. Helen has to tap the two women on the shoulder to get their attention, then she shouts over the clanging: 'I also heard that she ran off with him, but it turned out terribly. He left her in some motel in the west without anything. Of course she could have come home, but she felt too embarrassed and humiliated; she just couldn't face her sister who had been left with the children.'

Frankie and Taylor shake their heads. The conductors have

pulled the steps down and passengers begin to climb off. Helen checks over the bobbing heads for regular customers. As the small crowd makes its way up the stairs, Frankie starts in with, 'Taxi? Anyone needs a taxi?'

She gets three kids from the local college and an assistant professor, who won't let her carry his bag.

Taylor gets two middle-aged men who need to get across the bridge and another twenty miles beyond that. The whole trip will end up taking her an hour.

Helen has found a regular, an old man who has two people with foreign accents with him. She helps with their suitcases and smiles as she is introduced. The man's home is just outside the village; it will be an early evening.

One, two, three, like a parade the taxis pull out of the station and turn into the road heading to the village; in a mile or so, Taylor will turn off, then at the centre of town, Frankie will go left, Taylor right, ending their evening together.

Of course there was much truth in Helen's story about the woman left at the station; some years ago – more like forty than five or six – a man not from Arizona but Arkansas was arrested and convicted for suffocating a female hitch-hiker over in Ulster County. No doubt Helen was remembering this. Also her sister met a man, though not at the train station, rather at the Grand Union, while it was raining and her car would not start. He offered her a lift, within two weeks they were married and lived quite happily in Michigan where he was later transferred. He died just this year. And then, it was about seven years ago, when Helen went to meet her husband, Jim, at the station, though it wasn't the train that was late, rather it was Jim and he had missed it in New York – for reasons she learned to her misfortune only a month later.

He had tried to call home though, but she had been out visiting friends, so it wasn't until the last passenger was off, as she waited at the top step of the platform, that it dawned on her that he wasn't coming home that night. As she went to her car, a man was waiting at the taxi-stand; there being no taxi in sight. A lift was offered, why she did it she didn't know, he accepted; his hands were large and while shifting down into third, coming into the village, her hand touched his. She can tell you almost exactly at what stop on that road. She never had a drink with him, though he did ask, but she refused and went home; but soon she phoned the Inn where he did have a room, found him not in, hurried to the Inn, heard he had just been in the bar but had left, tried his room again, woke him up, apologised and went home. That was the entire story until Jim left her a month later, and this night became important and no doubt figured in her story.

They are nearing the old man's house, almost an estate, and as he points out the sights of the village moments earlier, he adds, 'Even our taxi-drivers. Look at her, besides being pretty, did you know Helen has a PhD? She could have a million jobs, but this is what she chooses to do.'

Helen puts the blinker on, they are turning into the driveway.

'Why is this?' asks one of the foreigners.

'I don't know,' Helen replies, 'I sort of like waiting around the station, and besides you never know who you're going to meet.'

'And take home!' the old man laughs.

'And take home,' says Helen.

THE WHITE CLIFFS

Mary Flanagan

Mary Flanagan was born in New England. She is the author of two novels, *Trust* and *Rose Reason*, and the short-story collection *Bad Girls*. She now lives in London where she is at work on a new novel.

'The White Cliffs' was first broadcast on Radio 4, read by Alice Arnold.

'What are you gaping at?'

'It's a valentine, isn't it?'

Auntie Lil squinted at the red paper heart I held up for her inspection.

'You been messing about on the sly?'

'No such luck. It's for Mr Papakiriacou. I found it just now in his trouser pocket.'

'The Greek?' she sniffed. 'Who'd send him a valentine I'd like to know.'

I could have made an educated guess. I'm real good at guessing. But I wasn't going to tell Auntie Lil. She thinks she's head of MI5 and it's her right to be kept informed.

'What's it say?' she suddenly called.

'Love from one who sees the beauty of your soul.'

'Well, his soul had better be beautiful because his face is nothing to write home about.'

'What would you know about souls?' I replaced the valentine in Mr Papakiriacou's aquamarine trousers. He might not be Mel Gibson, but he'd got something. He was very defined, if you know what I mean, like someone had outlined him in Biro. He had a big smile and soppy brown eyes and was sweet to the baby. And he'd always compliment me on my new perm or my leather skirt – things like that. His nose was – let's be polite – prominent. But I could understand what Mrs Tine might see in him.

Course my aunt wouldn't. Not that she's stupid. She's made herself a nice little bundle out of the White Cliffs Launderette. (She named the place after a rude weekend she spent on the south coast in 1971.)

How did I know Mrs Tine was the lovesick admirer? I watch people instead of the game shows and cartoons my aunt gapes at all day on that old black-and-white telly in the office. It's a boring job folding laundry, loading and unloading the machines. I need stimulation. So I get to know the customers. It's a real-life soap opera. Like I said, not much gets past me.

Except that valentine. How had she slipped it into his pocket without my noticing? Mrs Tine's not exactly foxy, and her grasp on reality isn't what I'd call strong. She's a nervy type. I sized her up for a loony tune the first time she came into the White Cliffs dragging a wicker shopping trolley that was leaking water all over the pavement.

'The washer's broken,' she gasped, nearly in tears. 'It died right in the middle of the rinse cycle. All my bedlinen.' She stood in a puddle fumbling with her change purse. Together we dragged out the dripping sheets and crammed them into the drier. While they went round and round she straightened her hair, which didn't make that much difference, and tried to calm down. Well, we started nattering and she told me she lived around the corner on Uffing Road. Uffing Road is one of those pedestrian streets being all tarted up. I walked along it every day on my way from the estate to the White Cliffs. The address and her accent convinced me she was all right for dosh. Not that her clothes gave it away. She must have been forty-five but had a wardrobe my Nan wouldn't have worn back in 1953.

So we're sitting chatting when in comes Papakiriacou, in a hurry for his laundry as usual. He drove a minicab and delivered and collected his clothes between fares. You always knew he was arriving because you'd hear one of those pirate Greek stations blasting away on his radio. I introduced him to Mrs Tine who was so polite it'd kill you.

'Where is your home, Mr Papakiriacou?' she asked.

'Cyprus,' he answered proudly. 'The birthday of Venus.'

'A lovely place.' She gave him a knockout smile.

'You are been?'

'Oh yes. We enjoyed it so much.' She actually blushed.

When he finally left, she stood at the window waving good-bye, and he waved back from the front seat of the car with its flashing red rose tied to the rear-view mirror.

Right away she starts pumping me for information, trying to be subtle and not succeeding. I told her he'd come to

London last October to drive for his cousin who ran the minicab company. He'd spend the winter here then go back to Cyprus when the tourist season started and his brother's restaurant opened. He sent all the money back to his wife and four kids.

'The Greeks work terribly hard,' Mrs Tine said.

I should have figured something was up when two days later she was back, this time with a couch cover and a counterpane. She claimed she was spring-cleaning, but it seemed a bit early in the year for that kind of thing. The following Thursday she was in again with the sheets she'd only just washed and which didn't look that slept in. The Zanussi still hadn't been fixed, she tells me. Repair men are so unreliable. Next time she's buying a Bosch. Well she sat there for two hours, her nose in the *Home and Freezer Digest*. Turns out she's a freezer freak and keeps it stocked like she's expecting war or famine or the Russian winter. She never cooks to eat, only to freeze, so she has to thaw every meal. She said it made her feel secure to see a fridge full of all those future dinners. I call it neurotic.

Still, Mrs Tine was a nice woman. She knit my Cynthia a hat with a pompom and gave her a Peter Rabbit mug for her first birthday. And she was nice as could be when Cynthia threw it on the floor and broke it. I felt sorry for her too. I met her husband who was a narrow-shouldered geezer with a fat bum. He had a head of fuzzy red-blond hair that looked like a panto wig, though it was all his own, I'm afraid, and a complexion like corned beef. And she'd had three kids by this bloke.

The next week she comes on a Tuesday. Machine still kaput, so she says. Like clockwork Mr P drops off his wash between fares. They act like they're long-lost friends. He enquires about her Zanussi like it's a dear relation. He kisses her hand and mine and drives off, illegal bazouki music all over the street.

'Does Mr Papakiriacou live locally?' she asks . . .

Well, no prizes for guessing that by the end of January Mrs T's turning up *only* on Tuesdays. Each time, she and Mr P would have a fussy, affectionate little exchange. Then she'd sit and stare at the same page in her *Home and Freezer Digest* for over an hour.

She was running out of excuses. The Zanussi couldn't be on the blink for ever, and her husband could easily have afforded the Bosch. All her underwear – which I bet you she normally washed by hand – was being ruined by the drier: elastic puckering, whites turning to dinge grey. She confessed she liked coming to the White Cliffs, me and my aunt were so friendly, she missed babies and adored my Cynthia, she'd become a home-body since the children went away to school. For a while I believed her. Okay, I thought, it's warm in here and she's lonely. Let her sit and dream about freezers. She's not doing any harm.

Then I found the valentine and my lightning brain saw the plot. But what next? Would Mr P follow up? And if he did, how could I make sure I knew about it? Like I said, the White Cliffs was a live soap opera, except I got to play around with the characters.

The Tuesday sessions got longer. All of a sudden they both had mountains of laundry to do. She must have stripped every room in the house, and he was doing his cousin's dirty socks as well as his own. They wouldn't let me touch it. Take a break, they'd say. You're on your feet all day. And they'd start slamming a small fortune in 50p's into the machines. I realised I was playing Cupid. I'm not as cynical as I make out.

'What we've got here,' said my Auntie Lil, 'is a proper courtship.' Then she gave them her office.

As you've probably guessed, they were not averse to this, and by the end of March were trysting on Tuesdays *and* Thursdays between two and four. Once when I'd been to a hen party the night before and was feeling rough, they offered to look after Cynthia while I had a quick kip. This too became a habit. They brought Cyn sweets and cuddly toys and she got completely spoilt. Not only were they courting, they were baby-sitting . . .

*   *   *

As far as I could tell, the lovebirds never did much more than hold hands and moon over each other. He was too religious and she was too proper. She could only be daring to a point. I said I felt guilty that so much of their precious time was spent preventing Cynthia from doing herself GBH, but they said they liked it. They were playing house.

Auntie Lil, who was that pleased with those 50p pieces, took advantage of the situation to nip across the street to the betting shop or into Zia's Mini-Market for a packet of fags. She got her highlights done and made a couple of shopping trips to Brent Cross. It was all super-convenient.

In late April, Mr P made his announcement.

'I have a community from my brother.' He whipped out a letter which he translated from the Greek. Most of it was incomprehensible, and Mrs T was catching every word like they were eggs that might fall on the floor and break. But the last line was all too clear.

'Restaurant open in two weeks. Return back fast please. Dmitri.'

Mrs T went the colour of her underwear. I felt sorry for the poor woman. My aunt felt sorry for Mr Papakiriacou. We all spent a lot of time feeling sorry.

That Thursday Mr P arrived with a purple-and-white rabbit for Cynthia. He gave Mrs T one of those big cameo pins they sell at Brick Lane market and she acted like it was the Kohinoor. Lil and I got two boxes of chocolate brazils. He kissed our hands, he kissed Cynthia's forehead. He kissed a tearful Mrs Tine on both cheeks. Then, weepy himself, he drove away, his red rose flashing, taking his beautiful soul with him.

No surprise, we didn't see much of Mrs Tine after that. The White Cliffs depressed her, she said. She was going back to her freezer.

I left the launderette in June. Cynthia was too hyper to take to work, so I was stopping at home until she was ready for playschool. Colin said what a good mum I was, but I couldn't pretend I was happy. Pretend isn't one of my strong points. I was bored, if you want to know. I missed Mrs T

and Mr P and the launderette soap operas. I even missed
Auntie Lil. Thing I hate most in the world's the feeling of life
going on without me. Maybe I'm not so different from Mrs
T, except I'm smart enough to keep clear of the love department. I like to keep my mood uppish.

So I strapped Cynthia in the pushchair and went to see my
aunt. In the office I found Mr Zia from the mini-market
reading the *Standard* while *The Young Doctors* played without the sound.

'Mrs Lillian has gone to Brighton for the day,' he beamed.

'And you're minding the shop?'

'No, no, no. I am visiting only.'

'Visiting who?'

'Mrs Tine. Do you know Mrs Tine?'

I certainly did, and in she walked with a cake she'd frozen
last year and thawed that morning.

'Hello, my dear. We've missed you.' She kissed me. 'Staying
to tea, I hope?'

Next morning I rang Auntie Lil, who'd had a late night
and was not best pleased.

'Why didn't you *tell* me about Mrs Tine?'

'Didn't know it was my job to keep you up to date. She
comes once a week. I need a day off. The pace gets to me.
I'm not what I was.'

'Rubbish. Anyway I'm talking about Mrs Tine and Mr
Zia.'

'They're an item.'

'Since when?'

'Since I found a valentine in Zia's pyjamas.'

'Not again!'

'Worked before, didn't it? But you got a lot of neck ringing
at seven when you never come round any more. Now let me
get my beauty sleep.'

I don't know what Spam-face thought about his wife's
working in a launderette. But they're still married, and she's
at the White Cliffs three days a week now. I'm a regular
visitor. We all drink tea and eat Mrs Tine's cakes. Mr Zia
doesn't join us now his wife's back from Kenya, but a nice

man who works in a Turkish restaurant on the Essex Road kept us company today while his wash was drying. *Scooby Doo* flickered away in a haze of static. Auntie Lil still has that old black-and-white telly. She refuses to trade it in. My aunt's a bit mean. That's why she's rich, I guess.

TELLING STORIES

Maeve Binchy

Maeve Binchy was born in Dublin. She worked as a teacher and later as a journalist for *The Irish Times*. Her short stories have been published widely and her major novels, extensively translated, include *Light a Penny Candle*, *Echoes*, *Firefly Summer* and *Circle of Friends*.

'Telling Stories' was first broadcast on Radio 4, read by Joanna Myers.

People always said that Irene had total recall. She seemed to remember the smallest details of things they had long forgotten – the words of old pop songs, the shades of old lipsticks, minute-by-minute reconstructions of important events like Graduation Day, or people's weddings. If ever you wanted a step-by-step account of times past, they said to each other: ask Irene.

Irene rarely took herself through the evening before the day she was due to be married. But if she had to then she could have done it with no difficulty. It wasn't hard to remember the smells: the lilac in the garden, the polish on all the furniture, the orange blossom in the house. She even remembered the rich smell of the hand-cream that she was massaging carefully into her hands when she heard the doorbell ring. It must be a late present, she thought, or possibly yet another fussy aunt who had come up from the country for the ceremony and arrived like a homing pigeon at the house.

She was surprised to hear Andrew's voice, talking to her younger sister downstairs. Andrew was meant to be at his home dealing with all his relations just as Irene had been doing. He had an uncle, a priest, flying in from the African Missions to assist at the wedding. Andrew's grandmother was a demanding old lady who regarded every gathering as in some way centring around her; Irene was surprised that Andrew had been allowed to escape.

Rosemary, her sister and one of the bridesmaids, had no interest in anything apart from the possible appearance of a huge spot on her face. She waved Andrew airily up the stairs.

'She's been up there titivating herself for hours,' Irene heard her say. Before she had time to react to Rosemary's tactlessness, Irene heard Andrew say 'Oh God,' in a funny, choked sort of voice, and before he even came into the room, she knew something was very wrong.

Andrew's face was as white as the dress that hung between sheets of tissue paper on the outside of the big mahogany wardrobe. His hands shook and trembled like the branches of the beautiful laburnum tree outside her window, the yellow blossom shaking in the summer breeze.

He tried to take her hand but she was covered in hand-cream. Irene decided that somehow it was imperative that she keep rubbing the cream still further in. It was like not walking on the crack in the road: if she kept massaging her hands then he couldn't take them in his, and he couldn't tell her what awful thing he was about to tell her.

On and on she went rhythmically, almost hypnotically, as if she were pulling on tight gloves. Her hands never stopped moving; her face never moved at all.

He fumbled for words, but Irene didn't help him.

The words came eventually, tumbling over each other, contradicting each other even, punctuated with apology and self-disgust. It wasn't that there was anyone else, Lord no, and it wasn't even as if he had stopped loving her, in many ways he had never loved her more than now, looking at her and knowing that he was destroying all their dreams and their hopes, but he had thought about it very seriously, and the truth was that he wasn't ready, he wasn't old enough, maybe technically he was old enough, but in his heart he didn't feel old enough to settle down, he wasn't certain enough that this was the Right Thing. For either of them, he added hastily, wanting Irene to know that it was in her interests as well as his.

On and on, she worked the cream into her hands and wrists; even a little way up her arms.

She sat impassively on her little blue bedroom-stool, her frilly dressing-table behind her. There were no tears, no tantrums. There were not even any words. Eventually he could speak no more.

'Oh Irene, say something for God's sake, tell me how much you hate me, what I've done to your life.' He almost begged to be railed against.

She spoke slowly, her voice was very calm. 'But of course

I don't hate you,' she said, as if explaining something to a slow-witted child. 'I love you, I always will, and let's look at what you've done to my life ... You've changed it certainly ...' Her eyes fell on the wedding dress.

Andrew started again. Guilt and shame poured from him in a torrent released by her unexpected gentleness. He would take it upon himself to explain to everyone, he would tell her parents now. He would explain everything to the guests, he would see that the presents were returned. He would try to compensate her family financially for all the expense they had gone to. If everyone thought this was the right thing to do he would go abroad, to a faraway place like Australia or Canada or Africa ... somewhere they needed young lawyers, a place where nobody from here need ever look at him again and remember all the trouble he had caused.

And then suddenly he realised that he and he alone was doing the talking; Irene sat still, apart from those curious hand movements, as if she had not heard or understood what he was saying. A look of horror came over his face: perhaps she did not understand.

'I mean it, Irene,' he said simply. 'I really do mean it, you know, I wish I didn't.'

'I know you mean it.' Her voice was steady, her eyes were clear. She did understand.

Andrew clutched at a straw. 'Perhaps *you* feel the same. Perhaps we *both* want to get out of it? Is that what you are saying?' He was so eager to believe it, his face almost shone with enthusiasm.

But there was no quarter here. In a voice that didn't shake, with no hint of a tear in her eye, Irene said that she loved him and would always love him. But that it was far better, if he felt he couldn't go through with it, that this should be discovered the night before the marriage, rather than the night after. This way at least one of them would be free to make a different marriage when the time came.

'Well both of us, surely?' Andrew was bewildered.

Irene shook her head. 'I can't see myself marrying anyone

else but you,' she said. There was no blame, regret, accusation. Just a statement.

In the big house, where three hundred guests were expected tomorrow, it was curiously silent. Perhaps the breeze had died down; they couldn't even hear the flapping of the edges of the marquee on the lawn.

The silence was too long between them. But Andrew knew she was not going to break it. 'So what will we do? First, I mean?' he asked her.

She looked at him pleasantly as if he had asked what record he should put on the player. She said nothing.

'Tell our parents, I suppose, yours first. Are they downstairs?' he suggested.

'No, they're over at the golf club, they're having a little reception or drink or something for those who aren't coming tomorrow.'

'Oh God,' Andrew said.

There was another silence.

'Do you think we should go and tell *my* parents then? Grandmother will need some time to get adjusted . . .'

Irene considered this. 'Possibly,' she said. But it was unsatisfactory.

'Or maybe the caterers,' Andrew said. 'I saw them bustling around setting things up . . .' His voice broke. He seemed about to cry. 'Oh God, Irene, it's a terrible mess.'

'I know,' she agreed, as if they were talking about a raincloud or some other unavoidable irritation to the day.

'And I suppose I should tell Martin, he's been fussing so much about the etiquette of it all and getting things in the right order. In a way he may be relieved . . .' Andrew gave a nervous little laugh but hastily corrected himself. 'But sorry, of course, mainly sorry, of course, very, very sorry that things haven't worked out.'

'Yes. Of course,' Irene agreed politely.

'And the bridesmaids? Don't you think we should tell Rosemary now, and Catherine? And that you should ring Rita and tell her . . . and tell her . . . that . . . well that . . .'

'Tell her what, exactly?'

'Well, tell her that we've changed our minds . . .'

'That you've changed your mind, to be strictly honest,' Irene said.

'Yes, but you agree,' he pleaded.

'What do I agree?'

'That if it is the Wrong Thing to do, then it were better we know now than tomorrow when it's all too late and we are man and wife till death . . .' his voice ran out.

'Ah yes, but don't you see, I don't think we *are* doing the Wrong Thing getting married.'

'But you agreed . . .' He was in a panic.

'Oh, of course I agreed, Andrew, I mean what on earth would be the point of not agreeing? Naturally we can't go through with it. But that's not to say that *I'm* calling it off.'

'No, no, but does that matter as much as telling people . . . I mean now that we know that it won't take place, isn't it unfair to people to let them think that it will?'

'Yes and no.'

'But we can't have them making the food, getting dressed . . .'

'I know.' She was thoughtful.

'I want to do what's best, what's the most fair,' Andrew said. And he did, Irene could see that, in the situation which he had brought about, he still wanted to be fair.

'Let's see,' she suggested. 'Who is going to be most hurt by all this?'

He thought about it. 'Your parents probably, they've gone to all this trouble . . .' He waved towards the garden where three hundred merrymakers had planned to stroll.

'No, I don't think they're the most hurt.'

'Well, maybe my uncle, the whole way back from Africa and he had to ask permission from a bishop. Or my grand-mother . . . or the bridesmaids. They won't get a chance to dress up.' Andrew struggled to be fair.

'I think that I am the one who will be most hurt.' Irene's voice wasn't even slightly raised. It was as if she had given the problem equally dispassionate judgement.

'I mean, my parents have other daughters. There'll be

Rosemary and Catherine, one day they'll have weddings. And your uncle, the priest ... well he'll have a bit of a holiday. No, I think I am the one who is *most* upset, I'm not going to marry the man I love, have the life I thought I was going to.'

'I know, I know.' He sounded like someone sympathising over a bereavement.

'So I thought that perhaps you'd let me handle it *my* way.'

'Of course, Irene, that's why I'm here, whatever you say.'

'I say we shouldn't tell anyone anything. Not tonight.'

'I won't change my mind, in case that's what you're thinking.'

'Lord no, why should you? It's much too serious to be flitting about, chopping and changing.'

He handed their future into her hands. 'Do it whatever way you want. Just let me know and I'll do it.' He was prepared to pay any price to get the wedding called off.

But Irene didn't allow herself the time to think about that. 'Let me be the one not to turn up,' she said. 'Let me be seen to be the partner who had second thoughts. That way at least I get out of it with some dignity.'

He agreed. Grooms had been left standing at the altar before. He would always say afterwards that he had been greatly hurt but he respected Irene's decision.

'And you won't tell *anyone*?' she made him promise.

'Maybe Martin?' he suggested.

'Particularly not Martin, he'd give the game away. In the church you must be seen to be waiting for me.'

'But your father and mother ... is it fair to leave it to the last minute?'

'They'd prefer to think that I let you down rather than the other way. Who wants a daughter who has been abandoned by the groom?'

'It's not that ...' he began.

'I *know* that, silly, but not everyone else does.' She had stopped creaming her hands. They talked like old friends and conspirators. The thing would only succeed if nobody had an inkling.

'And afterwards . . .' He seemed very eager to know every step of her plan.

'Afterwards . . .' Irene was thoughtful. 'Oh, afterwards we can go along being friends . . . until you meet someone else . . . People will admire you, think you are very forgiving, too tolerant even . . . there'll be no awkwardness. No embarrassment.'

Andrew stood at the gate of the big house to wave goodbye; she sat by her window under the great laburnum tree and waved back. She was a girl in a million. What a pity he hadn't met her later. Or proposed to her later, when he was *ready* to be married. His stomach lurched at the thought of the mayhem they were about to unleash the following day. He went home with a heavy heart to hear stories of the Missions from his uncle the priest, and tales of long-gone grandeur from his grandmother.

Martin had read many books on being Best Man. Possibly too many.

'It's only natural for you to be nervous,' he said to Andrew at least forty times. 'It's only natural for you to worry about your speech, but remember the most important thing is to thank Irene's parents for giving her to you.'

When they heard the loud sniffs from Andrew's grandmother, the Best Man had soothing remarks also. 'It's only natural for elderly females to cry at weddings,' he said.

Andrew stood there, his stomach like lead. Since marriage was instituted, no groom had stood like this in the certain knowledge that his bride was not just a little late, or held up in traffic, or adjusting her veil – all the excuses that Martin was busy hissing into his ear.

He felt a shame like he had never known, allowing all these three hundred people to assemble in a church for a ceremony that would not take place. He looked fearfully at the parish priest, and at his own uncle. It took some seconds for it to sink in that the congregation had risen to its feet, and that the organist had crashed into the familiar chords of 'Here Comes The Bride'.

He turned like any groom turns and saw Irene, perfectly at ease on her father's arm, smiling to the left and smiling to the right.

With his mouth wide open and his face whiter than the dress she wore, he looked into her eyes. He felt Martin's fingers in his ribs and he stepped forward to stand beside her.

Despite her famous recall, Irene never told that story to anyone. She only talked about it once to Andrew, on their honeymoon, when he tried to go over the events himself. And in all the years that followed, it had been *so* obvious that she had taken the right decision, run the right risk and realised that their marriage was the Right Thing, there was no point in talking about it at all.

MY GOOD FAIRY

Christopher Hope

Christopher Hope was born in Johannesburg and grew up in Pretoria. His books include *Moscow! Moscow!* and *My Chocolate Redeemer*. A new novel, *Serenity House*, will be published later in 1992 followed by a second collection of stories. He is a regular contributor to Radios 3 and 4 and now lives in London and Switzerland.

'My Good Fairy' was first broadcast on Radio 3, read by Tim Pigott-Smith.

Nicodemus was a big giver. And this was odd, him being so skinny. His tunic was cut square across his chest and there seemed next to nothing to the guy. Just these little arms and his legs in the long baggy shorts narrowing from the knee to little rocky ankles. His fuzz of black beard was blacker than his face. He didn't even have much to say, just 'yes' and 'no', and 'take this, my little lord'. He looked like nothing but then he'd wink or clap and suddenly something would appear.

He came with the house. If he hadn't coughed when we went into the garage, 'I'd never have found him!' my father told Gus Trupshaw. He was stored in the darkness along with a blue Rudge bicycle frame without wheels, a wooden clothes-horse, two broken ladders, a case of Trotter's Jellies 'from the heart of South Africa' – lime-green and as hard as cakes of soap because the damp had got to them – and an advertisement for New Consolidated Goldfields which included among its directors Sir G. S. Harvie-Watt, Bt., TD, QC, MP. I used to say the name to myself in all its crackling glory late at night when I was in bed and sleep wouldn't come and I thought of vampires and death.

Badminton had royal connections. All its sandy streets were named after English kings and queens: Henry Street and Edward Avenue and Charles Road. As a way of keeping up the connection the neighbours gave their dogs royal names: Nero and Genghis and Arthur. When my father was demobbed in 1946 he came home and bought a house on the new, ex-servicemen's estate. A raw development of spec houses set in rough veld. As if in a rage our fathers worked like furies with picks and shovels making gardens and rock-eries, often still wearing bits of their service gear, an Air Force cap, a Sam Browne, cursing the shale and the heat and the burglars. The burglars lived, everyone knew, in a patch of bluegums where the estate sloped into a little frothing river.

Beyond the river and the bluegums the iron-hard red ground stretched away to a range of hot, rough hills.

The burglars in the bluegums haunted the estate. Men slept with their service revolvers beside their beds. When butter and flour disappeared from pantries or booze vanished from liquor cabinets, people said their servants were related to the burglars and they whispered that the burglars were good at taking impressions of keys in cakes of soap. The dogs got bigger. Attila and Julius and Adolf slavered in the backyards. And when they found no burglars to bite, they bit the neighbours instead, or visiting aunts, or each other. Fathers leapt from their beds in the small hours and ran naked into the velvet African night blasting away with their pistols. I never saw a burglar. But I believed in them, the way I believed in God and Sir G. S. Harvie-Watt.

For the rest not much happened. There was a time when we thought that Mr and Mrs Strydom down the road had a leper working in their garden. And Maggie, one of my neighbours who was about nine, sometimes took off her clothes and ran around the house stark naked and we all tried not to look. On Wednesdays the water-truck came and the streets ran like rivers and we chased it barefoot and were happy. Nicodemus watched us and clapped his hands as if we were the best show on earth.

Then Margot Van Reen became a widow. She lived a few doors away with her husband Alec who had come back from the war a full lieutenant and began building a rockery along the front fence. He keeled over one day just as he was planting out some Namaqualand daisies for winter flowering.

My father blamed the government. 'That's what we get. The soldier's reward. This is a damn silly country. I went off to fight the Nazis and I came back to find that the place was being run by dyed-in-the-wool fascists. Thanks for nothing!'

It was at about this time that my father joined the Torch Commando. About twenty-five ex-soldiers who hated the dyed-in-the-wool fascists got together in secret and took to running through the estate after dark plastering letter-boxes with their emblem, a fiery torch which appeared to be growing out of an ice-cream cone. Everybody got up in the mornings and looked at the stickers on their letter-boxes and pretended to be mystified.

When Mrs Van Reen lost her husband she walked about in the rain without appearing to notice. She wore white a lot and with her blond hair and pale face this made her look as if she was made of mist. She never cleaned her windows. And if you met her in the street and said 'Good morning, Mrs Van Reen,' she would turn away and cry. And if you said 'How are you?' – she'd say things like 'I long for winter. Autumn was nearly the finish of me.' And then, if you really tried, and you said to her: 'Well, winter's not far away. We're in November already,' she would turn her face up to the sky, flutter her eyes, and her lips would move as if she was praying to someone.

'Feel free, Margot. Take him whenever the spirit moves.' My father had marched Nicodemus over to Mrs Van Reen's house and pushed him at her. 'He isn't trained for anything. But take him. With my compliments. He can do a bit around the house. Or in the garden. He's not the brightest but he's keen and he doesn't need anything.'

That was true. In his small room behind our garage he slept on a thin blue mattress on an iron bedstead. Two uniforms of white calico, big loose shorts, tunics cut square at the neck. Both tunics and shorts were edged in red piping. A mirror framed in red plastic hung from a nail and beside it he had pasted a photograph, cut from a newspaper, of Mussolini in military uniform.

'This is a happy, fat chap!' Nicodemus pointed at the dictator. Then he brought his own face close to his mirror. 'And this is a silly, thin chap.'

Nicodemus could only give. He had a force inside him that made him tend that way. It was like he had a list to starboard or a bad leg. He made and gave. Catapults were his speciality, the Y-piece cut from the green branch of the bluegum, stripped of its bark and then sun-dried. The rubber he took from old inner tubes and for a sling he took the tongues from his own sand shoes.

'My godfathers!' my mother cried when she saw him hobbling about in his tongueless shoes. 'That's the last time that I provide him with decent footwear!'

He loved French knitting. I wore a tall gum-pink hat around the estate for days until my mother told me to take it off because Mr Strydom said I was growing up like 'a pansy'. And then a few days later I ran into Lloyds Briggs in the dark little wood behind Swirsky's pharmacy and he cut open the back of my hand with a piece of glass, saying as he did so: 'That's what you get for wearing a pink hat.' I walked home to Nicodemus, not hurting much, but puzzled and rather worried about the blood splashing on my legs. He stopped the bleeding and bandaged it so beautifully I really did cry. When my mother saw me she screamed and marched me straight up to Swirsky for a professional opinion. 'I really don't know what this child has done to himself. Honestly, Martin! All this and Christmas almost on us. What will you think of next?'

Swirsky in his white coat, ironed wafer-thin, took off the wrappings and examined the wound. 'It's clean,' he pronounced, 'and the dressing is a beautiful job.'

'It ought to be,' my mother replied grimly, 'that was my best tea-towel. Irish linen, if you please. Thank you very much, Mr Nicodemus!'

'Who is Nicodemus?' Swirsky wanted to know.

'He came with the house,' said my mother. 'Are you travelling, Mr Swirsky?' It was rumoured that Swirsky went to Rhodesia at least twice a year.

'Home is where the heart is,' said Swirsky.

Whenever Nicodemus had done something beautiful he liked to go down on his knees, lean back and crouch on his haunches, blow out his cheeks and pop his eyes. I knew what he meant. The silly thin chap had become the happy fat chap – he had turned into Mussolini. He certainly got on with things at Margot Van Reen's place. He cleaned the windows and finished building the rockery while she watched from the kitchen window as if, perhaps, she expected the curse that killed her husband to fell Nicodemus too.

We invited her over for Christmas lunch and I remember how she smiled at my father across the turkey and said: 'Your Nicodemus! He's a champ!'

'I hope he's not giving you any trouble,' said my mother. 'Martin, sit up straight and try not to breathe when you eat. Nicodemus cooked our lunch. Mind you, I have to watch him every inch of the way.'

Nicodemus arrived with a plate of steaming pumpkin. Mrs Van Reen waved, a little windmill wave, as if she was polishing a mirror. Nicodemus showed his teeth through the steam, then he bowed with one hand behind his back and laid the plate in front of Margot Van Reen like a butler or a real waiter.

When he'd left my father said: 'He's not a bad old stick.'

'He's a dear,' said Margot Van Reen. 'He's my good fairy!'

Later that afternoon we all went to the Christmas party in the kindergarten. Mr Swirsky was always Father Christmas. At first there'd been some on the estate who'd objected to that because he was Jewish. But Swirsky said: 'Don't think of me as Jewish – I'm neutral.'

He looked fat and angry in his red robe and hood and woolly whiskers. 'I'll take Maggie first!' His grey trousers hung beneath the robe and in two minutes he was clipping people on the ear and shouting, 'If you kids don't shut up, I'll close the show!'

When Nicodemus turned up and sat at the back on the floor, Swirsky pulled off his hood and I saw how his own moustache refused to lie down under the cotton-wool moustache. Swirsky's own moustache was angry and sharp, like an assassin's knife.

'Sayonara!' He pointed at the door. 'Arrivederci!'

'Can I read my letter to Father Christmas?' Maggie wanted to know.

Everyone turned around. You could tell from his language that Mr Swirsky really liked to travel. His moustache looked sharper than ever. It seemed to be planning a war.

'He's not doing any harm,' the voice spoke from the back

of the room where all the grown-ups were standing. 'It's Christmas, Mr Swirsky.'

'No one invited him,' said Swirsky.

'I did,' said Margot Van Reen.

Without waiting to be told Maggie read her letter.

Dear Father Christmas,
Could you give me a tent and a sponge and a chair and a
skipping rope and that is all —

Love from Maggie

Swirsky pulled on his hood and hit his beard to make it stick. Then he pulled Maggie onto his knee: 'Waddya think this is – Christmas?' He gave her a beach ball. All the grown-ups laughed. All except Nicodemus who lifted his head like he'd seen a vision and tears poured down his cheeks.

'Oh happy days!' said my father. 'You can always depend on Nicodemus to fish up something from nowhere.'

It was some time in January when I met Mrs Van Reen in Henry Avenue. She was dressed in blue silk and winked at me: 'Nicodemus is building me a bower of bliss. I feel like the Lady of Shalott. I've felt that ever since Alec died: I've been pining for the return of my knight.'

By February it was there, a summerhouse, and Nicodemus had sunk the posts and set up a trellis and planted sweet peas and a creeper called Peachadilla which Mrs Van Reen said would flower in July. She sat in her summerhouse and drank tea out of small blue cups.

One evening I found Nicodemus lying on his bed wearing a full white beard which hooked on behind his ears. He was staring into the mirror and smiling. When he saw me he patted my hand. 'Happy! Happy, my little lord.' Then he rolled over again and stared into the mirror. His beard was fat and flowing. His eyes were wide. He looked at the picture of Mussolini and he looked at himself and I could see how happy he was.

Then the presents started appearing on the doorsteps in the mornings. There were French-knitted scarves; there were catapults and kites; there were reed flutes and little bicycles constructed from coathangers and they all came wrapped in Christmas paper. It was the paper Nicodemus had collected from the floor on the day that Mr Swirsky gave out the presents.

'Someone has it in for us,' said Gus Trupshaw. 'For God's sake, how can you have Christmas in February?'

'Gus, listen – can you imagine where we will be by July?' My father ran his finger across his throat. 'This is distinctly nasty.'

'Someone's got a damn nerve,' my mother said.

The Torch Commando sent for lights, they fetched the dogs, their torches burnt into the darkness and they were happy again. Suddenly they were out at night with a chance of catching all the burglars in the bluegums. It was a bit like the war – they were chasing Germans again. All the dogs which had bitten the neighbours and the aunts and each other now had something real to hunt. There were shots fired, though Gus Trupshaw said afterwards they'd been blanks.

They ran him to earth in Mrs Van Reen's garden. To escape the dogs he climbed on to the roof of the summerhouse and crawled to the edge and peered into the darkness. He kept his hand pressed to his forehead, trying to see beyond the bright torches.

Margot Van Reen ran out in a pink nightdress. She kicked my father, she bit Gus Trupshaw. But the hunters ignored her. They began shaking the trellis, they trampled the Peachadilla creeper; they snapped the sweet peas. And once they had him in hand they drove him away in a Morris Minor with a blanket over his head.

'To save him from the dogs,' said Gus Trupshaw.

'You bastards,' screamed Margot Van Reen. 'What have you done with his beard?'

But afterwards she seemed fine. She never mentioned Nicodemus. She started smiling. By July she was saying happily: 'Autumn is a lovely season, don't you think? So fruitful!' She wore red dresses and straw hats.

One day in July Swirsky came to see my mother and his

moustache was at its most dangerous. It was pressed to his nose like a pirate's throwing knife. He and my mother went into the kitchen and locked the door. As he was leaving the house I heard him say: 'I'm en route.'

My mother said quietly, 'Will she have it?'

'Too far gone to stop it. She came to the pharmacy wanting something for her swollen legs. Oh yes, she's having it and she's as pleased as punch. And she's staying.'

'And you're heading out?' my mother asked.

'Cape Town,' Swirsky said. 'It's just that I thought you should be told.'

'Why me?'

'Well, he was yours. It seemed right you should be the first to know.'

'I didn't ask for him,' said my mother very frostily. 'I told you before – he came with the house.'

She told my father, 'It's all very well for him. Swirsky can come and go as he pleases. He's a bachelor. But what about the rest of us?'

'Jesus wept!' said my father.

Every night I said my prayers to make it stop. I asked God. I asked Sir G. S. Harvie-Watt, Bt., of New Consolidated Goldfields. Meanwhile she got bigger and bigger. Nicodemus had left us something. We watched it. We looked away. But it wouldn't stop. It was something coming to us.

SEEING LONDON

D. J. Taylor

D. J. Taylor was born in Norwich in 1960. His short stories have appeared in the *London Magazine*, *PEN New Fiction*, volumes I and II, and *Best Short Stories 1990*. His second novel, *Real Life*, will be published in spring 1992.

'Seeing London' was first broadcast on Radio 3.

Bobby walked in front of us, stiffly, over the wet grass. Roxeanne said (it was a Sunday lunch party at somebody's house): 'I guess you were right when you said I needed someone to show me London: with you being at the office all day. But I never thought I'd find him just like that. Can you believe it? I'm sitting outside one of those pavement cafés in South Moulton Street when this guy comes up and says in the cutest English accent: "Excuse me, is this yours?" And it's that ivory comb you bought me, that time you took me round the antiques market in, where was it, Portobello. It just fell out of my bag. You ever hear anything so corny? Anyway, there's a spare seat at the table and pretty soon we're talking like old buddies and I suppose I must have said something about wanting to see the sights, because pretty soon he looks at me all serious and says: "Would *I* do? As a guide I mean" – still with that accent like Jeremy Irons. So I put on my best Manhattan voice – you know, that husky drawl you laugh at over the phone – and said: "So where are you taking me, honey?" Just like that.

'"Don't worry," he said. "I can show you London." And that was the time I thought I'd made a mistake, because usually when an English guy says he's going to show you London he means Westminster and the Tower and between you and me I don't ever want to see another Beefeater again. Anyway it was raining by then so I said, "Let's take a taxi." But he just looked at me and said, "What's wrong with your legs? It's not very far." He can be very authoritative, you know. So we started walking down through Soho looking in the shops and, boy, does he know his history. Do you know they call it Soho because they used to hunt foxes there and that was what the huntsmen used to shout? I asked Bobby how he knew about this and he said he read a lot and he was interested. I like it when people are modest like that. There are some guys would have given you a reading list. A bit later I had to go – you remember I was meeting you to go to the ballet? – but I gave him my address. Yeah, I know what you told me but I could see he wasn't a psycho or anything, and next morning a guy turns up on a motorbike with a dozen white roses and a note from Bobby saying can he see me again? Can you believe it? Just like a movie with Robert Taylor.'

Bobby lingered behind us at the bar, paying for the drinks. Roxeanne said (it was at a theatre in the Strand): 'Okay. I'd better be straight with you. I know I haven't been about much the last two months, but you see Bobby moved in a week ago and I thought I ought to stay around. Don't worry, it was my idea, well both our ideas, and anyway I was so angry with the way Bobby was treated by the guys in his house. You remember when I met him he lived in this place in Battersea? Anyway, last week somebody stole fifty pounds off the landlord and they decided it was Bobby and he had to leave. And Bobby knew it was one of the other guys but he's so straight he didn't want to say so. Can you imagine that? So when he turned up at the apartment with a couple of suitcases, of course I let him in. Not that I actually mind having him around the place. He's so considerate – not like some of your Englishmen – and boy, does he like doing it. I talked to my mother on the phone the other night and she told me I sounded tired. "You'd be tired as well if you were doing what I've been doing," I told her.

'Plus I finally got to find out what he does for a job. You know I always wondered why he was around in the afternoons but wouldn't phone for a couple of days? Well, it turns out he's an actor! Not in movies or anything like that, but TV ads. You know the ad where the guys are sitting there drinking coffee and the first one has to borrow the second one's fountain pen? Well, that's Bobby standing there in the background mixing a drink. I got him to tell me about it. He told me he'd been to RADA on some scholarship – but there weren't any proper jobs for actors over here so he had to do ads for coffee powder. Can you believe that? I told him he ought to come out to the States and try for the network shows and he said he'd think about it. He'd go down a bomb with that accent.

'And the joke of it is he isn't English. Not properly. It came out because I was talking a lot about Mom and Dad. I mean, I guess if your father teaches at Princeton and your mother went to Vassar you tend to talk about it. He looked serious, you know that way he has, and said did I want to hear about his family? Anyway it turns out that he's Greek Cypriot. His father came over here just after Independence and married an English girl. I guess I can relate to that, what with Mom's family coming from Athens. He's really serious about that side of his life. I mean, if he has a spare couple of weeks in the summer he goes back to Cyprus to see his cousins and stay on the farm. I said I might go with him this year – you know how I always got off on that primitive community thing – if I can square it with the faculty. Yeah, and that reminds me, I thought you said actors over here were dumb? Well, I took Bobby to this party the department had last week – the one I told you about where all the lecturers come along with their wives and it's all terribly *English* and cultured – and he really wowed them. Spent half an hour talking to the Professor about the novels of Anthony Powell. When we came out I said to him: "How come you know all that stuff?" and he just said – you know that way he has of turning his head when he looks at you? – "Oh, I have hidden depths."

'Plus I'm still seeing London. Bobby's very serious about that. Sometimes I get back to the apartment in the evening really exhausted. But Bobby just says: "I promised I'd show you London," and so we'll get up, go to Trafalgar Square, Piccadilly or someplace and just look at the lights going on and all the people. And he has these plans, you know, about the places I ought to see. I mean, last week he got me up at six to drive down to Greenwich Park and see the dawn come up. He says you get a light there like nowhere else in London.

We just had half an hour. Bobby had to get back for a shoot. Half an hour running around in the wet grass, playing hide-and-seek behind the trees. Bobby can be a real kid when he wants to – and you know, I couldn't remember a time when I was so happy . . .'

Bobby sat in the deck chair, staring silently at the newspaper. Roxeanne said (it was at our house one evening in summer): 'Yeah I know I didn't come to the concert last night with you and Sam like I said I would. I know I didn't phone you at the office like we arranged. But Bobby had these friends round and I figured I ought to stay home. It was my fault. He was going to take them to a restaurant. But I told him: "Listen sugar, this is a partnership, right, and if you want me to stay home and cook for your friends then I'm happy to do it." I did that jambalaya you had when you came over that time and hash browns. Anyway they all seemed to like it. Just some guys Bobby knows from acting. To tell you the truth, he doesn't really like them. He just says that if you're an actor you have to hang around with people, you know, so you can find out when the jobs are coming up. Actually Bobby hates all that. He said he felt morally degraded having to sit there, smile and listen to these asshole directors. I said, listen honey, you don't have to tell me about that, you should see how things are in the faculty, the way people hang around the Professor trying to kid him he's got a sense of humour. Still I agree with him about those guys. After the meal they just sat there round the table, wouldn't help with the dishes or anything. And then when they'd gone I found someone had stubbed a cigarette out in that Sèvres vase – the one Dad gave me a couple of years back. Bobby was really furious about that – and when Bobby gets mad with someone he gets mad. He said if he could find out who did it he'd make them apologise to me personally. If I hadn't stopped him he'd have telephoned everybody right there on the spot at two o'clock in the morning. So I said, forget it hon, it's just a piece of china. No need to worry yourself about it. But do you know

what he did? Next evening when I got back from the college
– you know I've been working late a lot trying to finish that
article on Robbe-Grillet – when I got back there is the most
beautiful, not to say expensive, porcelain dish lying on the
table and a note from Bobby saying he was sorry. Must have
cost two hundred, three hundred dollars. And you know how
broke Bobby always is . . .

'Which reminds me, I know it was all fixed and I know
I said I would and everything but we can't make it to your
picnic on Saturday. The fact is I said I'd get up early and
drive Bobby out to this shoot someplace in the country. I
mean, he has to be there at nine, and boy, don't we know
all about the transport system over here. So I reckon the
least I can do is to take him. Plus the really exciting thing
is that Bobby thinks it's his big break, yes sir, a whole
three-parter on TV. It might even get shown in the States,
Bobby reckons. He told me the plot, you know, one of
those mystery stories set in a country house, that Agatha
Christie thing. So, no more crummy ads for a while. He's
been working terribly hard, filming all week and there's
another week after this one. Anyway, we've got quite a
routine going. We get up at six, we have breakfast –
Bobby's so *English* about breakfast, bacon, eggs, the whole
caboodle – and drive down. And then in the evening I pick
him up and we head back into town for supper. I don't
know where Bobby gets his energy. After a day like that
I'd be ready to flake out, but no sir, not Bobby. He wants
to go out dancing, to the clubs, take in a movie. He's cute
about that. He says to me, "Don't think, do" – you know
how introspective I can get. And, Jesus, I get so tired
sometimes. Especially in the mornings. The mornings is
when he likes doing it, too. But then I reckon anything
that makes my Bobby happy is fine by me . . .'

Bobby wasn't there.

Roxeanne said: 'You know I never did like to bad-mouth
people, and I hate talking about Bobby behind his back, but
if I ever meet a guy with problems like that again then I'll

count myself unlucky. I mean, I didn't know there could be people that jealous. You remember Max. You met him that fall at my folks' place. I haven't seen him in years but he sometimes calls me up in the evenings, just to talk about old times. He has this associate professor's job at Syracuse now. Well, he called one evening and Bobby picked up the phone. As soon as he heard it was a man's voice he said: "Forget it, she's out." Just like that. Anyway, I played it cool. I told him: "Honey, you might be a little upset about something but Max is one of my oldest friends and I can't have you talking to him like that," and he apologised, but it kind of pissed me off all the same . . .

'. . . But between you and me it was the dishonesty I couldn't take, because as you know I have this thing about being honest in a relationship. I mean, when Bobby moved in I said: "Look honey, I want you to treat this place as if it was your own. Don't think you have to ask permission every time you want to take a shower." But boy, did he take me at my word. Sometimes I thought we were just throwing one big party for Bobby's friends. And then I started missing things. Just little things. You know that bracelet Mom gave me when I got my doctorate accepted? It couldn't have been worth more than a few dollars. I thought I must have just lost it, you know how good I am at losing things. Same thing happened when I started losing bills out of my wallet. Nothing major, just fives and tens, and I thought: Uh huh, you must have spent more last night than you thought. But then finally I reckoned I had to confront Bobby about this: "Look, sugar, I know this is a difficult thing for me to ask but I think you're stealing from me and I have to know why." And do you know what he did? He started crying. Just lay down on that sofa there and burst into tears, said I'd been so good to him and he felt so ashamed and could I ever forgive him? So I told him: listen, it doesn't matter. You know I'd have given you the money if you'd asked me, just don't ever lie to me. And after that everything was okay for a while . . .

'. . . But it was the stuff about the job that really threw

me. All that business about Bobby being an actor and waiting for a break. Well, let me tell you that Bobby had as much chance of being a star as I have of teaching semiotics at Yale. Straight up. I once went to see him in this play at some theatre in, where was it, Lewisham, just in a room over some pub, and you know it was pathetic? Like some kid in a high-school prom, screwing up his lines and looking sort of helpless and upset. What beat me was how seriously he took it. I mean, he really thought he was going to be Scofield or someone. And then finding out that all the stuff about the shoot in the country was just a fake. Just hanging around with the guys in the tape room and hoping that someone was going to give him a job. How can you respect someone who behaves like that?

'. . . The sex? Well, when you get to my age, honey, you can take or leave the sex, especially when it's coming courtesy of some gorilla who can't even wait for you to get your breath back. But do you know what really blew it? Do you know what really knocked it on the head? Last week, when I was really tired – you know I had to rewrite that Robbe-Grillet piece for the *Journal of Aesthetics* – well, one night Bobby says: "We'd better get up early tomorrow. I've got something really special to show you, somewhere you have to go if you're seeing London." So we got up – four, five in the morning, I can't remember, I was so bombed – and took this cab way out through the City. Someplace called Billingsgate – guys in white coats and stinking fish lying around in piles. Bobby was really excited. He was sort of *proud* of it, if you know what I mean. He said: "Isn't this great? Right out of Dickens. I bet you never saw anything like this before." And I said: "Let's get this straight. You're making me lose four hours' sleep just to see a *fish market*? Forget it." And after that I thought, this is it, this is the end, this is where I quit . . .'

Michael sat hunched over the chessboard, his forehead creased in concentration. Roxeanne said (it was a Sunday lunch party at someone's house): 'The thing I like about Michael is that he's got a sense of humour. I mean, there I was standing in this gallery looking at some great mess of colouring when this guy comes up and says: "Of course you have to realise that what the surrealists were trying to do was to paint without any effort, and we all know what *that* leads to." Now I thought that was really funny, especially as Michael really *knows* about art. I appreciate every Englishman you come across in a gallery tells you he's done three years at the Courtauld, but Michael's stuff . . . The other day he was showing me these book illustrations he's done – it's a project he's working on and you have to give him the third degree to get him to talk about it. And let me tell you, they're as good as any of that Aubrey Beardsley stuff you guys always go on about . . .

'. . . You mustn't ever tell him I told you this, but the first time I met him I thought he was gay! Something about the way he speaks. Yeah, I know when English people talk about art it's as if they were holding an egg in their mouths. Well, I won't go into details but let me tell you I was one hundred per cent wrong about that! Of course, Michael's very busy right now, finishing the book and everything. But in the evenings I go round there – he has the cutest little apartment in South Ken. We have supper. A helpmeet? This guy is a grade-A *cordon bleu* chef, honey, which makes a change from some people I could . . .

'. . . Bobby? Funny you should mention Bobby. I heard about him just the other day. Bobby's in jail someplace. You didn't know? Well, it turns out that when Bobby got together with those actor friends of his it wasn't just cigarettes they used to smoke, no sir. They reckoned when the police raided the place Bobby was staying they found enough dope to keep half of London high for a week. Nine months for possession with intent to supply. To tell you the truth I used to wonder about it when he was with me. I can remember one time picking up his jacket and watching the papers roll out onto the carpet . . . You know, I went down to Greenwich with Michael the other day: there was this gallery he wanted to go to. And we ended up in that park, you remember, that godawful park with all the trees and the dogshit. And I suddenly thought about Bobby and, do you know, it was as if it had never happened. Believe me, sugar, it was as if it had never happened at all.'

THE GREEN LINE

Romesh Gunesekera

Romesh Gunesekera was born in Sri Lanka. His stories have appeared in *The London Magazine* and on Radio 4. His collection *Monkfish Moon* was published in early 1992 and he is now at work on a novel.

'The Green Line' was first broadcast on Radio 4, read by Alfred Molina.

Franky and Stevie were cousins. Franky was an estate agent, Stevie a travel agent. Their two offices were next to each other on the Broadway, but the one intercommunicating door, painted green, was bolted and locked. Franky liked to be on his own.

If anyone asked Franky about his cousin he would pretend to be mystified.

'Stevie? Stevie who?'

Then if you explained he would slap his cheek. 'Oh, you mean Stephanou the travel agent? That's the one next door, you have to go round the corner I think to get in.'

Stevie, on the other hand, didn't indulge in such histrionics; he played it straight. He was younger. Slim, neat and always smiling, a figure from one of his Cyprus posters stepping out in canvas shoes to greet sunshine with lemons. If someone came into the travel agency looking for Franky he would take them to the window and draw a curve with his lightly tanned hand.

'Just out and around the corner. Easy. No problem.'

People liked him. They enjoyed his holidays. He was efficient and helpful. Business thrived.

Franky hardly noticed.

He was in his late thirties. A heavy man with a large pyramid body. He was usually in shirtsleeves, loosely rolled up.

His office was chaos: papers piled everywhere, filing cabinets bombed open, wicker chairs with the wicker working loose. Three desks covered in debris steamed with a constant stream of percolated coffee.

He had a couple of assistants who were reasonably competent. The business ticked over: properties came and went. But they were never rushed off their feet; Franky always had time to think and brood.

Although he said he no longer had much time for Cyprus, he often drew on his Greek connection, clearing in his mind

111

a direct line to the fifth century BC. This he did mostly after a couple of glasses of wine at the local Crouch End taverna where, as a single man, he did much of his socialising.

'That was the *good* life, you know,' he would say. 'Our Mediterranean climate, warm and healthy. A simple life: a bed, maybe a stone, to sleep on, meat to eat, wine and plenty of thinking.'

'But Franky, that is how it is *now*. For you,' Georgiou the proprietor would reply. He enjoyed talking to Franky.

'Ah Georgiou, you are wrong. That is how it *seems*. It is even how it *ought* to be. But it is very definitely not the way it is, my friend.'

Franky had learned his philosophy well. He could draw distinctions with a thumbnail.

'The kebab, I will grant you, is good. The wine, well we know our wine, it is also very good.' At this point Franky would tip back his glass and drain the last drops. 'So good we must have more.'

Georgiou would laugh and pour. He liked Franky. Franky reminded him of the past. Companionship. Old jokes. Speculation without responsibility.

'Also it is true that the *thinking* goes on.' Franky would tap his elongated head. 'But the *climate*, the climate, my friend, is very definitely different.'

'Yes. Very different.' Georgiou would pour more wine. Franky was a late luncher. Often he would be the last customer. Georgiou could afford to relax.

Under the influence of the local environment Franky would turn dialectical. The moment Georgiou agreed, Franky would change tack.

'That is not to say the climate here is bad. No, I think maybe this English climate is even better than that hot Mediterranean madness – sometimes.'

Although Franky thought deeply about many things, he ran his life, like his business, on principles of comfort and convenience. His island in the Mediterranean, the source of civilisation, had in his eyes betrayed him. Turned his childhood playground into a battlefield. Unlike Stevie, he had never been back to see what had happened.

Then, one day, Aphrodite appeared.

Aphrodite was in her mid-twenties. A bird-like, frail figure, she looked even younger. She had striking features: an attractive but curiously narrow face; her hair was coal black.

Franky had first noticed her when she had once gone into Stevie's travel agency. He thought he had also seen the two of them walking together and assumed she was another of Stevie's numerous girls. He was often to be seen escorting young women around the town. His hand would gently support the woman's elbow as he guided her along. His head, slightly ahead of them, inclined, would work a set of dazzling teeth through which, Franky was sure, the same conversation was offered time and again.

But then one day Aphrodite appeared in Franky's office. His assistants had finished early. It was a Saturday. Summer. She rang the desk bell in the front reception area. Franky was in his cubicle asleep after a heavy lunch. The bell was like a finger in his ear. He woke up irritated. Sweat ran down the furrows of his forehead.

Aphrodite stood in a white chiffon dress, smiling like a goddess. She took his breath away.

'I'm looking for a house.'

She tugged at her hair. Franky stared. Then, remembering his loose shirt, started to button up, elbows close in to cover the huge sweat-rings under his arms.

'Good, good. Please sit down.'

She surveyed the office. A concertina file fanned precariously on the nearest chair. Franky snatched it; the file yawned. Papers spilled.

'Please sit down,' he repeated.

She sat down with her feet drawn in while he collected the papers and crammed them back into the file. His head felt as spongy as the concertina – Georgiou's wine had not been at its best that day – and his thoughts crumpled in the same disordered fashion as the papers he stuffed.

'What kind of house?' he asked.

She said she wanted something for an elderly couple.

'Elderly couple?'

'Yes. Not for me.' She explained she was looking on behalf of a Mrs Kamal.

'Turkish?'

'Yes. Do you mind?'

'No, no,' he shook his head. He did not like to get involved in politics. His business was selling houses. He asked her if she was Turkish too.

'My mother is Turkish, my father Greek.'

'Impossible.'

She laughed.

The world was becoming more complex daily. He could hardly find his way. He emptied drawers looking for a house-list. Her eyes followed him everywhere.

The afternoon sun fell in pools inside the office; the temperature rose.

When at last he found the list he thrust it into her hands.

'Take this now. I'll send more later.'

'You know what we want?'

'Tell me.'

She told him. He took down all the details in his big scrawl on the back of a large manila envelope. When he looked up after he had finished their eyes met.

'Please help,' she said simply before she left.

That weekend he was tetchy. He felt like one of his clients in limbo, buying and selling a home. Unable to sit still. Fantasising. Going over and over the same conversation trying to work out the true meaning of such casually spoken words. Embroidering the memory with hints, suggestions, promises not recognised at the time. It had been a long time since he had been like this.

After a restless night, on Sunday morning, he decided he must go back to the office. He would work on the Kamal house. Relieve himself by doing something.

Until that weekend Franky had not believed in Sunday-working. He knew many estate agents did these days, like the one by the clock tower, but he thought it was crazy to do so.

'Would you work on Sundays?' he once asked his assistants.

The look of disbelief on their faces so mirrored his own feelings that he never broached the subject again.

This Sunday, however, his frame of mind improved with every step he took towards the office. The streets were deserted. It was early morning. The air still cool from the night.

He remembered the Troodos mountains for the first time in years. Cool air: the promise of sun. He used to go there as a child from Nicosia.

At the office door he hesitated and checked the street like a fugitive. The Broadway was deserted. He slipped in.

Although the room was exactly as he had left it the previous afternoon it felt strange. As if the turn of the earth had stirred the dust and changed the air. Stale but different. The light was weak. Shadows quivered. Franky headed for his cubicle.

He slumped down on his chair and searched his desk for another house-list. He found one and placed it in front of him. Next to it he placed his green felt-tip pen and a professional map showing his patch of north London: Finsbury Park to the North Circular.

He stared at these a long time. Then taking his pen drew a line across the map defining Aphrodite's region.

The green ink on the black-and-white street pattern was like the island maps that flashed back in '74. It triggered more emotions of his youth. He was in love during the war, the invasion. Far from the flames and the guns. It was a confusing time. The love didn't last long, but when it was over the war was over too. Division all round. Wounds everywhere.

He finished marking the map.

The next morning he handed it to one of his assistants.

'We need a house here,' he said, pointing at the green marks. 'Mrs Kamal. It is important.'

He didn't meet Aphrodite again all that week, but she was very much on his mind. He recognised the state. He brooded even more.

The next Sunday, a week after she had stepped into his office, they met in the grocery shop at the end of the road. He greeted her across the vegetables.

'Hello! How is it with Mrs Kamal?'

He was pleased to see she recognised him.

'We are trying. Your Nicky says it is not easy. And you? How are things?'

Franky shrugged. 'Life is like this. Getting on with getting on.'

Although he tried to sound philosophical he had been bothered all week with the image of her walking down the street with Stevie. The more he thought about it the less certain he became of what he had seen, and what he now imagined he had seen. Where were their arms?

'I think you are a friend of Stevie,' he blurted out.

'Stevie? Stevie who?'

'Stevie my cousin. Stephanou. The travel agent next door.'

'Oh I know who you mean. The *playboy*.'

Franky cringed. 'You are friends I think. Yes?'

'He did a holiday for me . . .'

'Cyprus?'

'No.' She selected some oranges. 'He is a friend of a friend. Why?'

'I just thought I had seen you before. With him.'

'Arranging the holiday I suppose.' She tasted a grape. 'Or maybe at his party at the beginning of the summer? I'd never been to a party so carefully planned. Seating plans! And those cigarettes. I never imagined that before in my life.'

Franky rubbed the back of his neck. 'What cigarettes?'

'He served cigarettes after dinner with the coffee, like cigars. But not in a packet. They came in little sprays in tiny silver cups. Like toothpicks. And I think he doesn't even smoke.'

'Stephanou likes to do things in the proper way.'

Aphrodite added lemons to her basket of fruit. 'Anyway I must go,' she said, and went.

The fruit in her hand took him back to his uncle's orchard that he had loved so much and so easily forgotten.

His uncle had been an extraordinary man. Aristotelian in

his ideas, Alexandrian in his actions. He was a polymath: an entrepreneur, an innovator, and a poet. He had a large family too, many children. Stevie. Franky felt so unaccomplished brooding his life among the red bricks and pebbledash of north London.

His uncle had loved to experiment. His orchards were magical. One never knew what would be growing there next. While everyone stuck to oranges and lemons he tried passion fruit and avocado. How had his uncle done so much, and he so little?

Perhaps, he thought, Aphrodite would be his turning point.

On his way home he passed the travel agency. Stevie was inside laughing and waving his gold-rimmed sunglasses in front of a girl. She too tipped back her head and laughed, fluffing a mane of coal-black hair.

Franky walked home thinking about the meaning of success.

Over the next few weeks Aphrodite popped in and out of the office, coffee percolated, papers drifted and other people's properties changed hands like dancers at a ball. Occasionally Franky would see her there; more often they would meet outside. At first by accident, then later it seemed almost a mixture of hope and design.

One day they met outside Georgiou's restaurant. It was Sunday. Lunch-time. She was examining the menu outside on the wall; dressed in a pink blouse and blue jeans. One foot was out of its shoe rubbing the back of the other leg as she read. Franky was wearing a new shirt: striped, casual, green.

'Good morning,' he said. 'Are you eating here?'

She turned round and smiled.

'I was trying to decide.'

'I can help you there. Easy. Maybe you will join me for lunch?'

Her jaw tightened. She took a deep breath.

'I eat here every day. I can recommend it.'

'Okay.'

Franky bowed slightly.

There was unconcealable surprise on Georgiou the

proprietor's face when Franky ushered her in. His eyes widened; he beamed even more than usual. Franky introduced the two to each other.

They went to Franky's usual table. A bottle of red wine was already there. Aphrodite slipped into Georgiou's place who discreetly left them. The blend of the past and the present, the familiar and the unfamiliar, was like a split of wine and sparkling water.

She ordered *keftedes*.

He ordered *afelia*.

They spoke about food. Franky about his taste for the simple; Aphrodite about her delight in spice and complexity.

'Is your mother really Turkish?'

She nodded. 'And you? Where do you come from?' she asked.

He told her about his family. His uncle's orange groves.

'You know Nicosia?'

'No,' she said.

'You have never been?'

'No, I haven't been to Cyprus. I would like to go someday.'

'I suppose I haven't for a long time. I don't know what is there any more.'

Hours seemed to pass in talking. Georgiou eventually started to draw the blinds. It was the first time Franky had talked so much to someone who was not Georgiou. He enjoyed it. She seemed pleased.

The next time they met they did it again.

Weeks passed, regularly they would lunch. Only the elusive Kamal house seemed to Franky to separate them.

Franky thought life was too two-edged. He prayed like a boy wishing.

'I understand,' he said, 'I understand now how my people really feel.'

Then one day when he came in, his assistant grinned.

'It's done.'

Franky's tired body straightened. His blood raced. Anything and everything seemed possible.

'Wonderful.'

He was beaming when Aphrodite came that afternoon.

'Mrs Kamal has a new home,' he said popping open a fresh pack of coffee.

She bit her lip. Her cheeks tightened, she broke into a smile and hugged him.

Coffee beans tumbled in the air.

Franky hammered back the bolts and unlocked the green door into the travel agency.

'Oy Stephanou, have you two tickets to Larnaca?'

MRS PULASKA

Christopher Burns

Christopher Burns is the author of three novels, including *The Flint Bed* (which was short-listed for the Whitbread Award for the best novel of the year) and *The Condition of Ice*. His short stories are collected in *About the Body*. He is married with two sons and lives in Cumbria. He is now completing his fourth novel, *Anvil Flatts*.

'Mrs Pulaska' was first broadcast on Radio 4, read by David Horovitch.

No one knew where she came from, or why she had sought refuge among us. Perhaps she yearned for the tiny villages and small farms of her childhood, now denied to her for ever by the forces of history; perhaps she merely sought escape.

For people such as us she was an emissary from an unknown world, a bizarre and oddly self-absorbed stranger with a heavy accent. The very planes and set of her face were different to the ones we were used to. She was angular, with bony features and protuberant eyes and long black hair like a witch's. For my schoolfriends and me she was a figure of both fear and scorn; we even imagined that she might be German, and to us all Germans were still enemies.

But her name was Mrs Pulaska, and she was Polish. Of Mr Pulaska, or of a wedding ring, there was no sign. For the time she was with us she lived in a tiny room at the back of the butcher's shop in the village. It must have been narrow and damp, but from the solitary window she could look out across the fields and towards the hills. Because she always looked cold and undernourished the shopkeepers gave her scraps of meat or the occasional vegetable, despite rationing. She wore black clothes even in summer, always with gloves; in winter she wore mittens, boots, and what looked like an outsize greatcoat scavenged from the remnants of an unidentified army.

When she began to come to our farm I felt both threatened and guilty. There had been no need for me to think such terrible things about Mrs Pulaska, I decided, for I feared that in some obscure way she had come to take revenge.

Instead she ignored me. She spent most of her time in the old barn my father rented her. She wanted to work in there, she explained.

I couldn't imagine what kind of work she would be doing in that cavernous and gloomy interior. The barn was no longer used; it was a relic from earlier days. My father always said that when better times came he would buy a prefabricated building, one that would cost little and be easy to maintain. Until then he was happy to let Mrs Pulaska use the old one. As soon as they had agreed the arrangement she painted the door a vivid fiery crimson.

So Mrs Pulaska, a bag slung over her shoulder, came down the muddy track from the village in all kinds of weather and went straight into the barn, closing the door firmly behind her. Often, too, I would see her scouring the hillsides, turning over stones as if she expected to find something hidden underneath them, or splashing calf-deep in water while she prodded at the streambed with a stick. Usually she would bring home a prize from these foraging missions, and return to the barn cradling a piece of limestone or quartz as if it was a precious object. Once she returned with a roll of discarded barbed wire. From within the secrecy of Mrs Pulaska's barn there came a series of noises which, although identifiable, only helped to create further mystery – a liquid slap and dribble, the rough scrape of heavy objects dragged along the floor, the wooden bangs of ladders or planking.

I asked my father what she was building. He told me that she was not a builder, but an artist. We were eating a meal. He spoke the word *artist* as if it was both a puzzle and an affront, and licked his fingers free of chicken fat.

'An artist?' I asked. For me, an artist was someone who drew the pictures in the *Beano* or the *Wizard*.

'If that's what she wants to call herself,' my mother said, 'then let her.'

'She's no more of an artist than I am,' my father said. 'She's just a crazy Polish woman, that's all.' Finished with his part of the bird, he threw the bones into the fire.

'But she's harmless,' my mother said. 'Just let her do what she wants to do. Why worry about what it is?'

My father grunted. He could tolerate only a little disagreement, and if my mother persisted he flew into a rage. I had often watched her abandon an argument because she hated his anger: usually I wished that she would stand up to him. The chicken bones, rich with fat, blazed and cracked.

Mrs Pulaska ignored me for months. I saw her in freezing slush, in sudden bright sunshine, in ceaseless rain, and always she had the same intent, preoccupied expression, as if the only things that mattered were held captive within her own imagination.

One day, however, she caught me spying on her.

My parents had agreed that we would leave her alone, and that we would not enter the barn. This made no difference to my father; he had no use for the building, and no interest in what she was doing. He only knew that it must be both temporary and irrelevant. But I was consumed by curiosity.

I had looked at some books in the tiny public library — books by artists. Inside their pages I found rich and luxurious images, lingering studies of disported flesh, sumptuous textures of limb, shadow, and hair. Quite suddenly I associated Mrs Pulaska with a kind of sensual comfort, and with nudity. It did not matter to me that I found her old, unattractive, bony, spare. Without warning she had become unnervingly physical, and I realised that her body must possess its own secret history, about which we knew nothing.

There was a slight gap in the barn door where the planking had shrunk. Furtive and eager, I pressed my eye to it.

I don't know what I expected to see; in the event, I saw nothing. A hessian bag had been fastened over the inside of the gap, blocking even a partial view.

As I stood back, crestfallen, Mrs Pulaska came round the side of the barn and bore down on me across the farmyard. The chickens scattered across the cobblestones.

I froze with guilt. She was wearing her greatcoat, which was torn and shabby by now, and her long hair trailed behind her like a sign of wickedness.

She put one hand on my shoulder — not hard, but my imagination turned it into a fierce grip. At several places her mittens had unravelled, and white skin showed through. She bent to look into my eyes. I thought she was going to hit me, and flinched. But instead she merely stared at me, as if I was an example of a species she had not noticed before. Then she let go and her mouth opened in a sad, lopsided smile. There was blood on her teeth.

She said something I could not understand, and her breath smelled of dandelions and earth.

'What?' I asked, my voice shaking.

She pointed at the barn and spoke again, but the vowels were hobbled and I could only pick out what I thought was the word 'wreck'. I nodded rapidly as if I understood, took a few steps to one side, then turned on my heel and raced away.

Now I began to notice that Mrs Pulaska was returning with other kinds of booty – shards of tile, the ribs and horns from sheep. She began to pester my mother for unwanted cutlery or broken glass. Or she would come up the lane with a borrowed wheelbarrow containing a hundredweight bag of plaster and a gallon tin of paint. When my father's friends arrived to slaughter our pig she watched with nervous dismay, and scurried out across the fields in a dismal, saturating rain rather than hear the animal killed. When it began to squeal she was a long way away, a scarecrow in a distant field, but I could still see her raise her hands to cover her ears. Afterwards, however, she asked if she could be given the bones and the skull.

Later that year a neighbour visited the farm with her small baby, and, in halting English, Mrs Pulaska asked to see it. My father was wary – the Polish woman coughed and spat a lot, he claimed. But the neighbour could see no reason to refuse. When Mrs Pulaska saw the child she reached out to hold it, and then withdrew as if all her nerve had unexpectedly vanished. She ran to her barn and secured the door behind her.

Afterwards, I heard the sound of a hacksaw grating through metal behind the red door. But in the pauses I could hear a high, stifled sound, only slightly more human. I walked away, not realising for some time that Mrs Pulaska was weeping.

Winter came early that year. Sleet drove from the skies for days on end; the rivers burst their banks and the lanes lay beneath water. Inside the farmhouse the fire burned constantly, and my father grumbled that the chimney should have been swept long before the weather had turned. We put log after log on the fire; even then, the walls dripped with condensation and the rooms all smelled damp.

My mother took pity on Mrs Pulaska. One morning she wanted to invite her to eat with us, but my father objected. The villagers had put an end to their charity, he told us. They all agreed that Mrs Pulaska might be poor, but that she could afford to feed herself. Instead of that she squandered her money on ridiculous things – builder's things. If she no longer had free food, then perhaps she would see sense.

Of course my father agreed with them.

'But she's ill,' my mother protested. 'Anyone can see that. All you have to do is look at her.'

'So let her feed herself and then go to a doctor,' my father said.

'Don't be heartless,' my mother said, 'the poor woman probably doesn't know what to do. Would *you* know what to do if you were ill in Poland?'

But my father was stubborn and bitter. 'It's not our fault that she's here. We're not to blame for what's gone on in Europe. Anyways, it's time she moved on from here. I told her she could only have the barn temporarily.'

My mother, colouring with anger, asked what he meant.

There was an envelope on the table where he did his paperwork. He tipped out its contents – several brochures, with plans and photographs of prefabricated buildings. 'That's what we need,' he said triumphantly. 'I always said it. Let's move with the times.'

'But Mrs Pulaska won't understand this,' my mother said. 'She probably didn't even know what "temporarily" meant. And she's still working in there.'

My father, angered at having his judgement questioned, strode to the door. 'I don't care if she's working. I don't care what she's doing. Because whatever it is, she'll have to stop. And I'll make sure she knows exactly what "temporarily" means.'

I sat looking at the fire because I did not want to look at my mother's face as she paced the floor.

After a few minutes she went to our front door. I followed, still not daring to look at her.

The farmyard lay under pools of water. My father, his face rigid with shock, was backing away from Mrs Pulaska, who was on her knees in front of him. Her black dress was spattered with mud and animal dirt, and her hands were held high in supplication. It was the first time I had seen her with bare hands; they were covered with white paint.

As we watched, my father took several steps backwards, and Mrs Pulaska pitched forward and sprawled across the muddy cobblestones like someone no longer able to walk. Suddenly she began to cough harshly and repetitively, as if she could not stop. From her lips there came a trickle of blood, bright as the paint on the barn door.

My mother ran across to the sprawled body. 'She needs an ambulance,' she told my father grimly, and he walked to the telephone as if under protest.

We carried Mrs Pulaska into the house and sat her in a chair in the warmest part of the room. I put another log on the fire while my mother wrapped her in a blanket. Mrs Pulaska had quietened now. She gazed ahead unseeingly, but her face twitched when the log's bark cracked as the flames took it. My mother wiped the blood from her chin, but as soon as she had done it a little more dribbled out of her mouth.

Mrs Pulaska's hands stuck out from under the blanket, and I saw that one of her wrists had something tattooed on it, a number that stood out in vivid purple lines against the bloodless skin. My mother reached forward and pulled the blanket across, as if she was covering something shameful. As she did we began to hear a muffled roaring noise; the soot in the chimney had caught fire.

My father looked outside. The wind had dropped, and smoke covered the farmyard in a greasy, swirling cloud.

We hardly spoke until the ambulance arrived. Mrs Pulaska

did nothing as she was carried into it, but merely stared at a horizon that was out of sight of the rest of us.

We followed my father across the farmyard and paused before the red door. 'She'll not need this any more,' my father said in the voice of a man finally proved right. He pushed the door open.

In the middle of the barn was a trestle-table, littered with implements – a chisel, paintbrushes, a heavy hammer. Half-opened bags of plaster and tins of paint were scattered around the table-legs. But it was the walls which had altered beyond recognition.

On them were figures, some of them painted, some of them built up in relief, all of them naked. Skeins of barbed wire threaded across and through them, and there was a subdued, ghostly glitter where the light caught tiny reflective fragments fixed into the vertical surfaces.

I was horrified and fascinated, and walked slowly round the walls. The more I looked, the more detailed and terrifying the work seemed. Here was a face with stones for eyes and teeth of rusted metal; here were children, their bodies dissected by hooks and claws. And here were tortured men with hearts of shattered tile, beaten women with skins of glass. The ribs of animals protruded from their chests, the skulls of beasts showed beneath the faces. A hundred or more tiny bones had been set into the plaster to look like the shadow of an infant. One figure reached out, its fingernails delicately fashioned from filed portions of horn, but its face was a mere daub of black paint in a white circle. Here there was no luxury, no pleasure; these people had no dignity, not even rest. If I had ever had doubts about their fate, these walls would have told me what it had been.

I came back to the door and stepped outside. I was trembling, and the smell of fire was in my nostrils.

'I don't understand this,' my father said.

Glowing flakes of soot drifted around me. 'It's a record,' I said.

He turned to my mother. 'I told you it would be worthless. The sooner we get rid of it, the better.'

He walked to the table and picked up the hammer.

My mother took him by the arm. I could see the force in her grip.

'Don't you dare,' she said.

JUMPING INTO BED WITH LUIS FORTUNA

Dilys Rose

Dilys Rose was born in Glasgow. Her work includes a collection of stories, *Our Lady of the Pickpockets*, and a poetry anthology, *Madame Doubtfire's Dilemma*. A second collection of stories is now being completed.

'Jumping into Bed with Luis Fortuna' was first broadcast on Radio 4, read by Maureen Beattie.

Dear Luis,
You don't know me and I hope you don't mind me writing
to you like this. You must have many admirers. I hope you
do. You deserve them. But if you really hate people posting
their opinions to you, please read no further. I just wanted
to say . . .

She scored through what she had written.

She didn't believe in heroes but still, in spare moments
downtown, she'd nip into bookshops in search of his latest
novel. Recently he'd become easier to track down. A prize-
winning film had been made of one of his books, and new
novels and reprints carried on the cover – along with the title
and his name, Luis Fortuna, in bigger print than previously
– the flier: Author of *Lair of the Panther Princess*. His titles
were always tacky or weird or misleading.

She'd got herself anchored: house, job, man, kids. The
backpack was long gone, she was well and truly stuck. To
compensate for her lack of mobility she watched travel pro-
grammes on TV, learned to cook Indian pastries and Mexican
soups, listened to music from Africa and Brazil and attended
a night class in Spanish.

Dear Luis,
You don't know me and I hope you don't mind me writing
to you out of the blue like this. I contacted your publishers
but they wouldn't give me your address. Maybe they
thought I was cracked or after money. I don't know, but
I expect you'll be pleased to know that you are being pro-
tected against that kind of postal nuisance. Anyway, they
suggested I sent a letter via their London office which
would then be forwarded to their New York office and on
to the capital city of the country where you are presently

living — they would not even tell me that! There, I was told, it would probably be held in a box for twenty-one days, when — if it had not been uplifted — it would be returned to sender or destroyed. So who knows whether this will ever reach you . . .

He was as much a vice as a pleasure. Some mornings, alone in the house, faced with unwashed dishes, unswept floors, unmade beds, the sight of someone's washing flapping above the back green in a good drying wind which shouldn't be missed, she'd let herself be seduced. Drawing the curtains, kicking off her shoes, she'd jump into bed with Luis Fortuna.

That was what it felt like, not just reading about some made-up characters, no, she was getting to know him personally, intimately. She had seen a couple of snaps on flyleaves. He was dark-haired, clean-shaven. Between his brows a small frown curled like a wormcast. Around his mouth was the hint of a smile, of mischief. That's what had got her hooked in the first place. When she put him aside and made a start on the beds or floors or dishes, it was with a vague thrill of guilt, as if she had not been in bed with a book, but a lover.

She wasn't a great reader, not like her husband John, a glutton for printed matter, consuming whatever he picked up at high speed. When she read at all she did it slowly, stubbornly, with resistance. Every so often she'd bring home the permitted quota of bulky hardbacks from the library. More often than not they were returned unread. Not that she had chosen rubbish, she was choosy, but most of the worthwhile stuff weighed on her, tired her out.

Luis Fortuna was a serious writer, no doubt about it. He didn't shy away from trouble, the agonies and slight aches, the huge and tiny tragedies, the depths and shallows. But he was funny. He could make her laugh out loud.

And he understood women so well, got under their skin, into their minds, didn't present them as saints or tarts, he was critical, bitchy, but there was an affinity, a relish for all their contradictions and subterfuge. Her husband was put off

Luis Fortuna by the trashy titles and lurid covers and she was glad. She had him to herself.

She imagined meeting him somewhere, anywhere would have done but she fixed on a terrace café, a sunny open place facing a busy plaza in an invented Rio or Buenos Aires. They'd sit under a spindly tree with small, fine leaves, watching other people. He'd be rude but charming. He'd catch the eye of rich, well-dressed women, purse his Latin lips then turn back to the table, take her hand in his and begin a sad but side-splitting story of a rich and well-dressed woman.

> *Dear Luis,*
> *I expect you receive a great deal of fan mail and perhaps you have an aversion to it. If so, please don't waste your time reading further because all I really want to say is that I've been reading your books for years and have found every one ... a real treat ... immensely satisfying ... an astounding feat of imagination ... compelling ... dazzling ... a winner ... deeply moving ... absorbing ... spellbinding ...*

She tried all kinds of stuff she had seen on the back covers, phrases taken from articles and reviews, phrases written by professionals, by people who had been paid for their words, and it all sounded inadequate or false. But she had to say something if she was going to write the letter at all, she couldn't write and say she'd read all his books without saying something. Version after version of the letter was scored through, crushed, binned. What she ended up with was:

> *Dear Luis,*
> *I just wanted to say that I think your books are great. Please write more.*

Such a skimpy note didn't seem enough to send by itself, halfway round the world. She'd send him a present. Christmas was only a few weeks away and by the time a parcel reached its destination it could merge with the seasonal mail.

But what to get for a man twice her age, a man she'd never met – except on paper and that fragmentally, enigmatically – what to give her hero?

Men were always difficult to buy for. Even John, whom she thought she knew inside out, even he was a problem when it came to presents: novelty gifts got him worried about hidden meanings; personal luxuries were scorned as extravagance; practical items – tools, kits, gadgets – were met with more immediate appreciation but ended up cluttering kitchen cupboards; clothes were hopeless. Though he moaned enough about what he had to wear, her attempts to brighten up his wardrobe had always failed: some detail – buttons, cuffs, collar, lapels – which she had overlooked, relegated the garment to years in a drawer.

Through green silk jungle fronds, a black, gold-eyed panther snarled out from the rack of paisleys, florals and polkadots, incisors gleaming, claws extended. The tie was almost as lurid as the cover of *Lair of the Panther Princess*. Luis Fortuna would love it. Or at least get a laugh. It weighed next to nothing, was easy to package, unbreakable. And on sale.

It was all ready to go: the note slipped inside crinkly tissue, the parcel wrapped, brown-papered, an additional note to the publisher clipped to one corner, the encompassing Jiffy bag stamped, addressed, sealed, hidden. She didn't want a lecture from John on the futility of spending good money on a complete stranger. Out of sight, out of mind and the daily battle to keep domestic muddle at bay resumed its stranglehold on her attention. News stories hit the headlines and slipped off the back page before she'd caught sight of them.

She unfolded the newspaper cutting which John had tucked under the teapot. A weather forecast? Two boxes – AFTERNOON and NIGHT. Small maps of the UK, scattered with clouds, directional arrows indicating winds and the occasional sunshine sputnik. Lighting-up and High-tide Times, Motorway Information and Satellite Predictions. A typical Met. Office report. Nothing out of the ordinary – no felt-tip arrows or stick figures or messages. Normal conditions for the season. Snowclouds looming over the north, motorway fog warnings, a sunny patch around the south-east. What was she missing?

She turned the paper over and saw it, the thick plain type-face, the solid black word: OBITUARY.

... from complications resulting from a minor operation, Luis Fortuna, best known for the highly successful film of his novel ... a small-town boy from a Pampas town ... a homosexual who never hid behind the skirts of an ideol-ogy ... died a dollar millionaire ... was going through a bad patch with José, his rough young lover.

He would write no more books. Her free time would never be the same again. There was nothing to be done and no use blaming herself for being lazy or indecisive or reticent, it wouldn't have made any difference to anything. And maybe she'd got him all wrong anyway. It had never occurred to her that he might be, might have been, gay.

She held the proof in her hands. She was settled and he was dead. It hurt, finding out hurt, not loud, public pain but an emptiness, an absence. This was it. There would be no spectacle on his behalf. He was not a president, a rock star, a magnate. Perhaps a biography would appear, an unfinished novel, but otherwise it was finished.

Christmas morning begins too early. The kids can't contain their excitement: it cracks and fizzles through the house. It's as well to postpone breakfast and get going on the presents: two big piles for Kate and Josie, two small bundles for Mum and Dad, a growing mound of discarded wrapping on the carpet. John picks up a small, neat package. Wearing an enthusiastic smile, a fatherly pretence, he tugs patiently at the knotted gold twine.

John wears his tie for Christmas. Throughout the day, as they act out their synchronised roles as parents, doing what they can to make the day pass peacefully – playing with the kids, taking a walk to the swingpark, cooking, eating and clearing up the dinner, slumping in front of Disney reruns — she catches sight of John as he stops in front of mirrors to admire his reflection. She too is surprised. She finds her husband strange, attractive.

THE BISHOP'S LUNCH

Michèle Roberts

Michèle Roberts is half French and lives in London. Her stories have been widely published and her last book of poems was *Psyche and the Hurricane*. She is currently in the middle of writing her seventh novel.

'The Bishop's Lunch' was first broadcast on Radio 3, read by Samantha Bond.

The angel of the resurrection has very long wings. Their tips end in single quills. The angel of the resurrection has three pairs of wings that swaddle him in black shawls, then unwrap when he needs them. The angel of the resurrection flies in the darkness. He is invisible and black. His feathers are soft as black fur.

That is what Sister Josephine of the Holy Face was thinking early on that Wednesday morning of Holy Week, four days before Easter. Whether or not her picture of the angel was theologically sound, she decided that she would record it later on in her little black notebook, the place where she was required to write down all her faults. These were then confessed at a weekly interview with the Novice Mistress. The black notebook was one of the few items Sister Josephine had been allowed to bring with her from home when she entered the convent. Her mother had put it in her suitcase herself, along with a new missal and four pairs of black woollen stockings.

One thought she knew not to write down in the black book was that she ought to be called Sister Josephine of the Unholy Stomach. At home, on the farm in the richly green countryside of the *pays de Caux*, she had drunk her breakfast *café au lait* from a china bowl stencilled with blue flowers. She had eaten warm crusty bread fetched half an hour before from the village bakery. On Sundays there was hot chocolate after High Mass, with *brioche* or *galette*, and a heavy appetite seen as a good thing. Here in the convent on the outskirts of Rouen, the day-old bread was always stale, and the thin coffee bitter with chicory and drunk from a tin cup.

Angels, having no bodies, were not tormented by memories of *saucisson* and cold fresh butter, of thick sourish cream poured over cod and potatoes, over beans, over artichokes. Yet the black feathers of the wings of the angel of the resurrection were very soft.

141

Sister Josephine was down on her hands and knees in front of the cupboard under the big stone sink of the convent kitchen, groping inside it for the bread-knife she had mislaid. Her fingers closed over a bunch of silky plumage. It wasn't an angel's wing, she discovered when she brought it out, but the feather duster she had lost a fortnight ago. Her penance for that had been to kiss the ground in the refectory before breakfast every day for a week. It had tasted of floor polish, and so had her food afterwards.

The bell rang for chapel. Sister Josephine spotted the bread-knife hiding behind a bucket of washing-soda. She flung it, together with the feather duster, onto the wooden table. Then she straightened up, untied the strings of her heavy blue cotton apron, and hung it on the nail behind the door. Not *my* apron, she reminded herself: *ours*.

She glided along the dark cloister as rapidly as she dared. She wasn't supposed to begin her kitchen duties so early, but she'd wanted to get on with slicing up the long *baguettes* into the bread-baskets ready for breakfast. There was too much work in the convent kitchen for one person to do, even in such a small community, but it would be a sin against obedience to complain. Putting Sister Josephine in sole charge of the cooking, the Novice Mistress had announced six weeks earlier, was a real test of her faith – and of the nuns' digestions, Sister Josephine had muttered to herself.

She knelt in her stall, amongst the other novices, yawning as she tried to follow the still unfamiliar Latin psalms. Her empty stomach growled. She clasped her hands more tightly together. They smelled of carbolic soap. They looked like her mother's hands: red, roughened by work. Her mother's hands were capable, quick and deft, as they needed to be for the labour of the farmyard and the house. Sister Josephine's mother was an expert cook. She was famous among the village women for the lightness of her *choux* pastry, the *gougères* and *éclairs* she turned out on feast-days and holidays. She made cider and Calvados from the apples in her orchard, and her cows produced rich sweet milk from which she skimmed off the thick cream she used in her cooking.

142

Sister Josephine had resisted all her mother's attempts to teach her the domestic arts. She had refused to believe that God wanted her to serve him through topping and tailing beans and cleaning tripe and peeling potatoes. She'd hungered for transcendence. She'd come to the convent to get away from the farm. Not to learn how to *cook*.

So, what in heaven, Sister Josephine asked herself for the hundredth time that Lent, am I going to do about the Bishop's lunch?

It was an ancient tradition in the convent, dating back to the days of the Foundress three hundred years earlier. Every year on Easter Sunday the Bishop of the diocese would say High Mass in the convent chapel and then join Reverend Mother and the nuns for their midday meal. To celebrate the end of the rigorous fasting of Lent and the presence of such a distinguished guest, and, of course, the resurrection of the Saviour from the dead, an elegant array of dishes was served. Sister Josephine knew that the Bishop, like all holy men of the cloth, had renounced the pleasures of the flesh, but nonetheless he would expect to be given exquisite food, just so that he could demonstrate his indifference to it as he ate.

Help me, she prayed.

The problem was two-fold. One: the nuns were much poorer than usual this year, having had to get the roof mended after the violence of the winter storms. Two: Sister Josephine was a clumsy and indifferent cook.

Help!

Normally she did not bother God with her problems over lost feather dusters and bread-knives and how to turn a handful of carrots and turnips into a nourishing stew for twenty hungry nuns. God was above such trivia, she was sure. But the Bishop's lunch was an emergency. God, normally occupied with wars, famines and disasters, would somehow have to be persuaded to descend to kitchen level.

The smell of incense made her open her eyes. Morning Mass had begun. She hadn't even noticed. Another fault to note down in her little black book. She reached into the skirt pocket of her habit, drew it out, and opened it hastily at random, pencil at the ready. Then she drew in a sharp quick breath of surprise, and bit hard into the top of the pencil.

Maundy Thursday passed peacefully, apart from the gardener reporting to Reverend Mother that someone had taken his rusty old rifle from its usual place in the shed, and that someone else had thoughtfully weeded all the wild sorrel from under the apple trees in the orchard.

On Good Friday the gardener told Reverend Mother he'd heard rifle-shots in the field backing onto the kitchen garden. Also, the traps he'd set for rabbits, all three of them, had been sprung by some wretched poacher. And when he went to investigate a great squawking in the chicken shed, he found that the best layers among the hens had been robbed of all their eggs. There would be none to take to market the following week.

Reverend Mother sighed. She consoled the gardener as best she could, and then sent for Sister Josephine. How, she enquired, did the young novice plan to manage making a lunch on Easter Sunday fit for a bishop to eat? 'I have been asking,' Sister Josephine replied, 'for a miracle.' Reverend Mother tapped her on the shoulder: 'Well, then, you'd better get down to some serious praying.'

Throughout that Good Friday afternoon the nuns knelt in the gloomy chapel, all its statues shrouded in purple draperies and all its candles extinguished. The chaplain recited the solemn liturgy of the Passion. Christ was stripped and scourged, crowned with thorns, and finally nailed to the cross. The nuns sang the great dialogue of the Church, taken from the Old Testament, between Christ and his people, a powerful lament of repeated longing and reproach. Rain beat at the chapel windows. Christ cried out for the last time and then died. The nuns filed out to their cold and frugal supper.

On Holy Saturday Christ was in the tomb and Sister Josephine was in the kitchen beginning her preparations for the Bishop's lunch. Swathed in her big blue apron, she scrubbed the table, the sink, the floor. Then, on the table, she laid out her *batterie de cuisine*: wooden spoons and egg-whisks; mixing-bowls; sharp knives; and a butcher's cleaver.

144

The rabbits she had taken from the gardener's traps were hanging in the pantry. Swiftly she skinned them, chopped them up and threw them into a pot with a bunch of herbs and half a bottle of Communion wine she'd filched from the sacristy after morning Mass. She fetched the pigeons she'd shot with the gardener's rifle two days earlier, plucked and trussed them, and arranged them on a bed of sliced yellow apples in a well-buttered dish. Finally she prepared a small mountain of potatoes and leeks, washed a big bunch of sorrel and patted it dry in a cloth, and checked that the two-dozen eggs she had removed from the hens were safe in their wicker basket in the larder.

When the knock came on the back door of the kitchen she darted across to lift the latch. She smiled at the boy who stood there, at the silvery aluminium churn he clasped in his arms and the squat bottle sticking out of his pocket. The boy's eyes were as blue as hers, his nose as aquiline, his chin as determined. They kissed each other on both cheeks. Sister Josephine took the churn and the bottle, smiled goodbye to the boy, and shut the door on him. Now everything was as ready for tomorrow as it could possibly be.

Early next morning, just before dawn, the nuns gathered outside the chapel in the darkness to witness the lighting of the new fire, the symbol of renewal and hope. They processed into the dim and silent chapel. The huge Paschal candle, studded with nails and flowers, could be anointed and blessed and lit. Now the risen Christ could blaze in the black night and drive away the shadows. Easter Sunday had arrived. The chapel could be filled with flowers and lights, the dark coverings taken off the statues, and the altars hung with lace and gold-embroidered cloths of white brocade.

The Bishop, with his retinue, arrived to say High Mass. The organ pealed; the nuns stood up very straight in their stalls and sang a loud hymn of praise: Christ is risen, Christ is risen, alleluia. The miracle of the resurrection was repeated in the Mass: through the actions of his chosen priest Christ offered his body, his blood, to nourish his children. The Bishop's hands moved deftly amongst his holy cutlery and crockery, wiping the chalice, picking up the silver cruet of water and wine, spooning more incense into the swinging gold boat.

Alleluia, sang the nuns: Christ has leapt from the tomb.

In the kitchen, Sister Josephine's *choux* pastry leapt in the oven.

The Bishop's lunch was an unexpected success, all the nuns later agreed. The rabbit *pâté*, scented with cognac and juniper, was exquisite. So too was the dish of roasted pigeons with apples and butter and Calvados, the sliced potatoes and leeks baked with cream, and the poached eggs with sorrel sauce. But, they unanimously declared, the *pièce de résistance* of the entire meal was the creation which ended it: an angel sculpted from *choux* buns stuck together with caramel and then coated with dark bitter-chocolate cream. A very noble confection, even the Bishop was heard to declare. Truly, said the nuns, a miracle.

After finishing the washing-up Sister Josephine opened her black notebook and studied again, gratefully, the recipes her mother had written down at the back of it, and which she herself had discovered only four days ago. Perhaps, she thought, my vocation is actually to train as a chef and run my own restaurant.

THE CREAMERY MANAGER

John McGahern

John McGahern's last novel, *Amongst Women*, was short-listed for the Booker Prize in 1990 and his short stories have appeared in numerous anthologies. At present he is preparing *The Collected Stories*, which will be published in autumn 1992.

'The Creamery Manager' was first broadcast on Radio 4, read by the author.

The books and files had been taken out. They hadn't yet stopped him from entering his office. Tired of sitting alone listening to the rain beat on the iron, he came out on the platform where he could look down on the long queue of tractors towing in the steel tanks, the wipers making furious, relentless arcs across the windscreens as they waited. He knew all the men sitting behind the glass of the cabs by name. That he had made his first business when he came to manage the creamery years before. Often on a wet summer's day, many of them would pull in below the platform to sit and talk. The rough, childish faces would look up in a glow of pleasure at the recognition when he shouted out their names. Some would flash their lights.

Today no one looked up. He could see them observing him in their mirrors after they had passed. They probably already knew more precisely than he what awaited him. Even with that knowledge he would have preferred if they looked up. All his life he had the weakness of wanting to please and give pleasure.

When the angelus bell rang from Cootehall, he began to think that they might have put off coming for him for another day, but soon after the last stroke he heard heavy boots crossing the cement. A low knock came on the door. Guard Casey was in the doorway but there was no sign of the sergeant. Guard Guider was the other guard.

'You know why we're here, Jim,' Guard Casey said.

'I know, Ned.' Quickly the guard read out the statement of arrest.

'You'll come with us, then?'

'Sure I'll come.'

'I'm sorry to have to do this but they're the rules.' He brought out a pair of bright handcuffs with a small green ribbon on the linking bar. Guider quickly handcuffed him to Casey and withdrew the key. The bar with the green ribbon

149

kept the wrists apart but the hands and elbows touched. This caused them to walk stiffly and hesitantly and in step. The cement had been hosed clean but the people who worked for him were out of sight. The electric hum of the separators drowned their footsteps as they crossed to the squad car.

In the barracks the sergeant was waiting for him with a peace commissioner, a teacher from the other end of the parish, and they began committal proceedings at once. The sergeant was grim-faced and inscrutable.

'I'm sorry for that Sunday in Clones,' the creamery manager blurted out in nervousness. 'I only meant it as a day out together.'

The grimness of the sergeant's face did not relent; it was as if he had never spoken. He was asked if he had a solicitor. He had none. Did he want to be represented? Did he need to be? he responded. It was not necessary at this stage, he was told. In that case, they could begin. Anything he said, he was warned, could be used against him. He would say nothing. Though it directly concerned him, it seemed to be hardly about him at all, and it did not take long. Tonight he'd spend in the barracks. The cell was already prepared for him. Tomorrow he'd be transferred to Mountjoy to await his trial. The proceedings for the present were at an end. There was a mild air of relief.

Less than a month before, he had bought stand tickets for the Ulster Final and had taken the sergeant and Guard Casey to Clones. He already knew then that the end couldn't be far off. It must have been cowardice and an old need to ingratiate. Now it was the only part of the whole business that made him cringe.

They had set off in the sergeant's small Ford. Guard Casey sat with the sergeant in the front. They were both big men, Casey running to flesh, but the sergeant retained some of an athlete's spareness of feature. He had played three or four times for Cavan and had been on the fringe of the team for a few seasons several years before.

'You were a terrible man to go and buy those stand tickets,

Jim,' Casey had said for the fifth time as the car travelled over the dusty white roads.

'What's terrible about it? Aren't we all Ulster men even if we are stranded in the west? It's a day out, a day out of all our lives. And the sergeant here even played for Cavan.'

'Once or twice. Once or twice. Trial runs. You could hardly call it *played*. I just wasn't good enough.'

'You were more than good enough by all accounts. There was a clique.'

'You're blaming the selectors now. The selectors had a job to do. They couldn't pick everybody.'

'More than me has said they were a clique. They had their favourites. You weren't called the boiler for nothing.'

A car parked round a corner forced the sergeant to swerve out into the road. Nothing was coming.

'You'd think the car was specially parked there to deliver an accident.'

'They're all driving around in cars,' Casey said, 'but the mentality is still of the jennet and cart.'

It had been a sort of suffering to keep the talk going, but silence was even worse. There were many small flowers in the grass margins of the roadside.

They took their seats in the stand halfway through the minor game. There was one grace: though he came from close to Clones, there wasn't a single person he knew sitting in any of the nearby seats. The minor game ended. Once the seniors came on the field he started at the sudden power and speed with which the ball was driven about. The game was never close. Cavan drew gradually ahead to win easily. Such was the air of unreality he felt, of three men watching themselves watch a game, that he was glad to buy oranges from a seller moving between the seats, to hand the fruit around, to peel the skin away, to taste the bitter juice. Only once did he start and stir uncomfortably, when Guard Casey remarked about the powerful Cavan fullback, who was roughing up the Tyrone forwards, 'The Gunner is taking no prisoners today.'

He was not to be so lucky on leaving the game. In the packed streets of the town a voice called out. 'Is it not Jimmy

McCarron?' And at once the whole street seemed to know him. They stood in his path, put arms around him, drew him to the bars. 'An Ulster Final, look at the evening we'll have, and it's only starting.'

'Another time, Mick. Another time, Joe. Great to see you but we have to get back.' He had pushed desperately on, not introducing his two companions.

'You seem to be the most popular man in town,' the sergeant said once they were clear.

'I'm from round here.'

'It's better to be popular anyhow than buried away out of sight,' Casey came to his defence.

'Up to a point. Up to a point,' the sergeant said. 'Everything has its point.'

They stopped for tea at the Lawn Hotel in Belturbet. By slipping out to the reception desk while they were eating he managed to pay for the meal. Except for the sergeant's petrol he had paid for the entire day. This was brought up as they parted outside the barracks in the early evening.

'It was a great day. We'll have to make an annual day of the Ulster Final. But next year will be our day. Next year you'll not be allowed to spend a penny,' the sergeant said, but still he could see their satisfaction that the whole outing had cost them nothing.

Now that the committal proceedings were at an end an air of uncertainty crept into the dayroom. Did they feel compromised by the day? He did not look at their faces. The door on the river had to be unlocked in order to allow the peace commissioner to leave and was again locked after he left. He caught the sergeant and Guard Casey looking at one another.

'You better show him his place,' the sergeant said.

To the right of the door on the river was a big, heavy red door. It was not locked. Casey opened it slowly to show him his cell for the night.

'It's not great, Jimmy, but it's as good as we could get it.'

The cement floor was still damp from being washed. Above the cement was a mattress on a low platform of boards. There was a pillow and several heavy grey blankets on the mattress.

High in the wall a narrow window was cut, a single steel bar in its centre.

'It's fine. It couldn't be better.'

'If you want anything at all, just bang or shout, Jim,' and the heavy door was closed and locked. He heard bolts being drawn.

Casually he felt the pillow, the coarse blankets, moved the mattress, and with his palm tested the solidity of the wooden platform; its boards were of white deal and they too had been freshly scrubbed. There was an old oil can beside a steel bucket in the corner. Carefully he moved it under the window, and by climbing on the can and gripping the iron bar he could see out on either side: a sort of lawn, a circular flower-bed, netting-wire, a bole of the sycamore tree, sallies, a strip of river. He tried to get down as silently as possible, but as soon as he took his weight off the oil can it rattled.

'Are you all right there, Jimmy?' Casey was at once asking anxiously from the other side of the door.

'I'm fine. I was just surveying the surroundings. Soon I'll lie down for a while.'

He heard Casey hesitate for a moment, but then his feet sounded on the hollow boards of the dayroom, going towards the table and chairs. As much to reassure Casey as from any need, he covered the mattress with one of the grey blankets and lay down, loosening his collar and tie. The bed was hard but not uncomfortable. He lay there, sometimes thinking, more of the time with his mind as blank as the white ceiling, and occasionally he drifted in and out of sleep.

There were things he was grateful for . . . that his parents were dead . . . that he did not have to face his mother's uncomprehending distress. He felt little guilt. The shareholders would write him off as a loss against other profits. The old creamery would not cry out with the hurt. People he had always been afraid of hurting, and even when he disliked them he felt that he partly understood them, could put himself in their place, and that was almost the end of dislike. Sure, he had seen evil and around it a stupid, heartless laughing that echoed darkness; and yet, and yet he had wanted to love.

He felt that more than ever now, even seeing where he was, to what he had come.

That other darkness, all that surrounded life, used to trouble him once, but he had long given up making anything out of it, like a poor talent, and he no longer cared. Coming into the world, he was sure now, was not unlike getting into this poor cell. There was constant daylight above his head, split by the single bar, and beyond the sycamore leaves a radio aerial disappeared into a high branch. He could make jokes about it, but to make jokes alone was madness. He'd need a crowd for that, a blazing fire, rounds of drinks, and the whole long night awaiting.

There was another fact that struck him now like coldness. In the long juggling act he'd engaged in for years that eventually got him to this cell – four years before only the sudden windfall of a legacy had lifted him clear – whenever he was known to be flush all his loans would flow back as soon as he called; but when he was seen to be in desperate need, nothing worthwhile was ever given back. It was not a pretty picture, but in this cell he was too far out to care much about it now.

He'd had escapes too, enough of them to want no more. The first had been the Roman collar, to hand the pain and the joy of his own life into the keeping of an idea, and to will the idea true. It had been a near thing, especially because his mother had the vocation for him as well; but the pull of sex had been too strong, a dream of one girl in a silken dress among gardens disguising healthy animality. All his life he had moved among disguises, was moving among them still. He had even escaped marriage. The girl he'd loved, with the black head of hair thrown back and the sideways laugh, had been too wise to marry him: no framework could have withstood that second passion for immolation. There was the woman he didn't love that he was resigned to marry when she told him she was pregnant. The weekend she discovered she wasn't they'd gone to the Metropole and danced and drank the whole night away, he celebrating his escape out to where there were lungfuls of air, she celebrating that they were now free to choose to marry and have many children: 'It will be no Protestant family.' 'It will be no family at all.' Among so many disguises there was no lack of ironies.

The monies he had given out, the sums that were given back, the larger sums that would never be returned, the rounds of drinks he'd paid for, the names he'd called out, the glow of recognition, his own name shouted to the sky, the day Moon Dancer had won at the Phoenix Park, other days and horses that had lost – all dwindling down to the small, ingratiating act of taking the sergeant and Guard Casey to the Ulster Final.

The bolts were being drawn. Casey was standing in the doorway. 'There's something for you to eat, Jimmy.' He hadn't realised how dark the cell had been until he came out into the dayroom, and he had to shade his eyes against the light. He thought he'd be eating at the dayroom table, but he was brought up a long hallway to the sergeant's living quarters. At the end of the hallway was a huge kitchen, and one place was set on a big table in its centre. The sergeant wasn't there but his wife was and several children. No one spoke. In the big sideboard mirror he could see most of the room and Casey standing directly behind him with his arms folded. A lovely, strong girl of fourteen or fifteen placed a plate of sausages, black pudding, bacon and a small piece of liver between his knife and fork and poured him a steaming mug of tea. There was brown bread on the table, sugar, milk, salt, pepper. At first no one spoke and his knife and fork were loud on the plate as the children watched him covertly but with intense curiosity. Then Casey began to tease the children about their day in school.

'Thanks,' he said after he'd signed a docket at the end of the meal which stated that he had been provided with food.

'For nothing at all,' the sergeant's wife answered quietly, but it was little above a whisper, and he had to fight back a wave of gratitude. With Casey he went back down the long hallway to the dayroom. He was moving across the hollow boards to the cell door when Casey stopped him.

'There's no need to go in there yet, Jimmy. You can sit here for a while in front of the fire.'

They sat on the yellow chairs in front of the fire. Casey spent a long time arranging turf around the blazing centre of the fire with tongs. There were heavy ledgers on the table at their back. A row of baton cases and the gleaming handcuffs with the green ribbons hung from hooks on the wall. A stripped, narrow bed stood along the wall of the cell, its head beneath the phone on the wall. Only the cell wall stood between Casey's bed and his own plain boards.

'When do you think they'll come?' he asked when the guard seemed to have arranged the sods of turf to his satisfaction.

'They'll come some time in the morning. Do you know I feel badly about all this? It's a pity it had to happen at all,' Casey said out of a long silence.

'It's done now anyhow.'

'Do you know what I think? There were too many spongers around. They took advantage. It's them that should by rights be in your place.'

'I don't know . . . I don't think so . . . It was me that allowed it . . . even abetted it.'

'You don't mind me asking this? How did it start? Don't answer if you don't want.'

'As far as I know it began in small things. "He that contemneth small things . . ."'

'Shall fall little by little into grievous error,' Casey finished the quotation in a low, meditative voice as he started to arrange the fire again. 'No. I wouldn't go as far as that. That's too hard. You'd think it was God Almighty we were offending. What's an old creamery anyhow? It'll still go on taking in milk, turning out butter. No. Only in law is it anything at all.'

'There were a few times I thought I might get out of it,' he said slowly. 'But the fact is that I didn't. I don't think people can change. They like to imagine they can, that is all.'

'Maybe they can if they try hard enough – or they have to,' Casey said without much confidence.

'Then it's nearly always too late,' he said. 'The one thing I feel really badly about is taking the sergeant and yourself to the Ulster Final those few Sundays back. That was dragging the pair of you into the business. That wasn't right.'

'The sergeant takes that personally. In my opinion he's wrong. What was personal about it? You gave us a great day out, a day out of all our lives,' Casey said. 'And everything was normal then.'

That was the trouble, everything was not normal then, he was about to say, but decided not to speak. Everything was normal now. He had been afraid of his own fear and was spreading the taint everywhere. Now that what he had feared most had happened he was no longer afraid. His own life seemed to be happening as satisfactorily as if he were free again among people.

Do you think people can change, Ned? he felt like asking Casey. Do you think people can change or are they given a set star at birth that they have to follow? What part does luck play in the whole shemozzle?

Casey had taken to arranging the fire again and would plainly welcome any conversation, but he found that he did not want to continue. He felt that he knew already as much as he'd ever come to know about these matters. Discussing them further could only be a form of idleness or Clones in some other light. He liked the guard, but he did not want to draw any closer.

Soon he'd have to ask him for leave to go back to his cell.

YOU AIN'T HEARD NOTHING YET

Jonathan Treitel

Jonathan Treitel was born in London in 1959. He has worked as a physicist in California and has a doctorate in philosophy. His short stories have appeared in various publications and on BBC Radio. His second novel will be published in spring 1992.

'You Ain't Heard Nothing Yet' was first broadcast on Radio 3, read by Andrew Sachs.

I was as far away from Charlie Chaplin's mouth as I am from yours. His thin lips would flicker on the screen above my head, his square moustache would pump up and down, while I would declaim in my most formal tone: 'I love thee for ever, my dearest.' Then the daffy blond floozey whom he was addressing would retort, 'Nay, thou lovest me not, thou drunkard.' I would speak on her behalf too. She would slap his cheek: he would tumble backwards.

I was not an 'actor'. I did not present myself in some false pose. I wore a simple white yukata and, in my dark recess beneath the bright screen, I was invisible to the audience. My art was purely to provide voices: a steady bass for the hero and a clear falsetto for the heroine. I was the Chief Speaker at the Superama cinema on Winter Crane Boulevard in Yokohama.

True, I did find myself making slight movements in accord with the action on the screen. I spoke the man's part with my head facing right; female, left. When Chaplin fell on his bottom, I crouched fractionally. When he performed a somersault, the little finger on my right hand twirled in a full circle.

I might compare my art with Sumo. The wrestler has but an instant to make a move at his opponent, to grab his belt or slap his belly. Once that moment of suspense is over, the rest is a formality; he will win or lose rapidly by one of the seventy-nine approved methods. And, so, if I observed, for instance, Chaplin's mouth about to open – the corner muscles wrinkling, the moustache lifting – I had to speak. Usually I found the right words, for I have a thorough understanding of the Western temperament, but on occasions I would misjudge: I might cry out in anguish while Chaplin's shoulders were shaking with laughter. Then I would have to alter my voice quickly but in a natural-seeming way. Fortunately, Westerners are notoriously and emotionally volatile.

My only view of the film was by means of a tilted concave

mirror. Sometimes, staring at this gave me terrible headaches and I could continue the performance only by numbing the pain with a bottle of scotch.

Certain scenes or actions were unsuitable for a Japanese audience, so the Manager would excise them. The heads of Douglas Fairbanks and Mary Pickford are coming closer, closer . . . then suddenly they are parting with tears of joy. I would cover the jump-cut with some murmured polite phrase.

Genuine Westerners were among my admirers. The resident foreign community of merchants and bankers would often attend the Superama. Most of them understood enough Japanese to appreciate my art. But there was always the danger that an American ship might come into port. The first I would know of it would be during the screening itself. I would be crouching in my recess, meditating before the performance, then I would notice a group of foreign sailors, drunk, staggering down the aisles. Their unruly hair would wobble across their foreheads. Some of them were ghost-coloured; others' skins were black. They would slouch near the front of the auditorium. All through the performance they would chuckle in the wrong places. They would recite the captions out loud. Most disconcerting of all, they would sometimes burst out laughing an instant *before* I declaimed the joke.

I consoled myself by thinking that all true artists must suffer. The artist must refine and perfect his art until the enactment is exquisitely boring. Despite this, each perform-ance must carry a genuine chance of failure.

But let me tell you what was most agonising. You might think Chaplinesque slapstick was tough, but I assure you that passionate love scenes were far worse. After speaking Valentino in a run of *The Sheik*, the doctor ordered me to lie down in a dark room for a week and communicate only by gestures.

When I recovered, the Manager welcomed me back to the Superama with a grand Western-style handshake. 'I've got a special treat for you tonight,' he said. 'Stay behind after the last show.' He smiled broadly and flashed his gold tooth.

I was not sure if this was a punishment or a reward. I dutifully waited in the auditorium late that night. I sat near the front. I was joined by the Chief Greeter who performed an elaborate bow. He nudged me and sniggered.

The Manager waved from the projectionist's cubicle. Light flickered on the screen. He came down the aisle, bearing an ice-bucket filled with assorted bottles, glasses and cocktail garnishes. He arranged himself and his drinks between me and the Greeter.

What we saw on the screen was grotesque. It had been composed, I had to admit, with a modicum of artistry. The Greeter had spliced together scenes cut from Hollywood films. First, there was a sequence of public nose-blowings. Douglas Fairbanks wiped his nostrils. Charlie Chaplin blew extravagantly into a huge white handkerchief. Mary Pickford wiped her tears away and snorted delicately. The Greeter was guffawing and the Manager was tittering. I did my best to make noises of merriment.

We drank pink gins, martini cocktails, whisky sours, and other elaborate concoctions whose names I do not know.

Then the film descended into pornography. No less than nineteen separate explicit mouth-to-mouth kisses, thirteen of them in close-up. I'm no prude. Photographs of such activities were readily available in Yokohama; in my youth I myself had not disdained them. Often, in the course of my strolls in the port area, I had seen prostitutes kissing their clients. But it was quite another thing to view osculation in motion, vastly magnified on the screen.

The finale was a lengthy interaction of Valentino with some anonymous starlet. The kiss lasted hours. We men were slurping our cocktails and choking with nervous laughter.

Then, behind us, we heard a high, clear giggle. We looked round. It was the Usherette.

The Usherette was a 'modern woman'. (That was the English term which she used to describe herself.) She whitened her face with powder. She lipsticked her mouth in a Cupid bow. Her hair was tied with red ribbon in two bunches at the back. She was wearing her favourite kimono made of organdie in a Liberty print. She was gazing at the image of Valentino's lips.

The Manager yelled at her, 'This is not for women! Go away and jump in the sea!' He threw a glass of neat gin at her.

She bowed politely and retreated.

A year later, I had the first premonition of doom. The largest rival cinema in Yokohama, the Abraham Lincoln Movie House near the harbour, had just installed the Vitaphone system. They were advertising a film called *The Jazz Singer*, which was supposed to have sound as well as pictures.

The Manager summoned me into his office. The Usherette and the Greeter were already there, standing at the back. The Manager addressed us:

'My dear comrades, we live in a time of peril. Our beloved cinema is under threat. I'm sure I don't need to spell it out.'

'Al Jolson,' the Usherette murmured.

'So there is only one thing to be done. We too must show *The Jazz Singer*!'

'But we don't have the system,' I said. 'We don't have the Vitaphone.'

'The Greeter will explain our strategy.'

The Manager gestured to him, and the Greeter began to talk in a loud lecturing voice.

'We have here a sound-producing machine.' He pointed with his chin at a desk in the corner, where reposed a Bakelite-and-steel contraption. I recognised it as a Victrola gramophone. 'Courtesy of the Usherette,' he lowered one eyebrow at her, 'we have obtained a recording of songs by Mr Jolson.' He pointed at a record in a white paper sleeve lying beside the gramophone. 'You, my dear Speaker, will operate the machine in synchrony with the film. *The Jazz Singer* will be screened at the Superama on the very same night as at the Lincoln!'

I was briefly relieved; then despairing. 'But . . . my Voice?'

The Manager said, 'I've telegraphed the distribution company in Tokyo. Apparently there's speech as well as singing in the film. In English, of course.'

'But I don't . . . That is to say, I do speak a *little* English. But —'

'Good, good,' said the Manager.

He took a pair of tickets from his desk and handed one to me and one to the Usherette.

'You will attend the premiere at the Lincoln. You, Speaker, will learn the voices. You, Usherette, will explain the English to him.'

'You understand English?' I asked the Usherette, surprised.

'*I sure do*,' she replied in English. 'I attend tea dances at the Bristol Hotel on a regular basis. The American sailors there say I'm the best quickstepper east of Pearl Harbor.'

Two days later, the Usherette and I were in the back row at the Lincoln. I was concentrating hard, memorising the correlation of sound and pictures. Every so often, I would scratch the back of her wrist, and she would whisper to me the meaning of some English phrase.

It was a celebratory occasion. The rows in front of us were packed with the elite of Yokohama in their finery. The foreigners were especially noticeable: consuls in black suits and stiff collars, Russian refugee ladies wearing their most elaborate imitation jewellery. It sickened me — all this ceremony just to welcome a mechanical product. Yes, the interplay of sound and sight in *The Jazz Singer* was precise and intricate, but every showing of this film would be exactly the same. True art is not about repetition but about subtle variation. There is no art unless each performance is a new, daring challenge.

Jolson began to sing about love.

The Usherette tapped her left foot in tempo.

Jolson ran forward and shouted something I could not understand.

I tapped the Usherette's wrist.

She mouthed, '*You ain't heard nothing yet.*'

'What?'

165

'I can't explain now. Later . . .'

After the film was over, we walked back together along White Crane Boulevard, beside the tramway. The performance of *The Jazz Singer* at the Superama was scheduled to begin in half an hour. I sipped rum from my hip-flask.

'Well!' she said.

'Yes.'

'Well . . .?'

'*You ain't heard nothing yet?!*'

She explained that sentence word by word. I still couldn't make much sense of it; it seemed a contradiction or a tautology. Besides, it was ungrammatical English.

My puzzlement must have shown because, as we were about to enter the lobby of the Superama, she turned to me and whispered, 'You poor thing. I'll make an American of you yet.'

I bowed from the neck up.

She leaned forward. Her scarlet lips were slightly parted. They touched mine very gently and backed away.

The brittle black disc settled on the Victrola's turntable. I fitted the playing needle in the groove. The automatic winding mechanism was primed. I uncapped a bottle of gin and a bottle of vermouth and arranged them on either side of the gramophone so that, if I felt the need during the show, I would be able to swig alternately and make a martini cocktail inside my throat. I closed my eyes and meditated.

The cinema was full. I heard that murmur of conversation you always get before a performance, rising and falling like the sound of the sea. I heard the click of heels as the Usherette glided up and down the aisles in her elegant way, vending ice-cream, salted beans and cigarettes. I heard a crowd of American sailors near the front, jeering and burping beer. I heard a little scream. I opened my eyes. A sailor was pinching the Usherette's bottom. She trod hard on his toes.

The house lights dimmed. The screen flickered above my head and reflected off the slanted mirror. I pressed a lever.

The Victrola began to emit a tinny jazzy music. The audience clapped.

I turned the gramophone on and off throughout the film, doing my best to synchronise sound and sight. Of course I could not achieve the perfection of the Vitaphone system, but since most of the audience had never attended a 'talkie' before, they cheered enthusiastically each burst of jazz. The sailors seemed rather bored by it all; no doubt 'talkies' had been screened in America months or years earlier. They drank much beer.

The moment I had been dreading approached. Soon, Al Jolson would zoom into close-up and speak, and I would have to imitate his voice. I took a long gulp of gin, then vermouth, then gin again, then vermouth again. Images swam in the tilted mirror. My head throbbed. Jolson jumped forward and opened his arms wide. I too found myself advancing one step with extended arms. '*You ain't heard nothing yet!*' he yelled. My mouth emitted a Japanese phrase, so ultra-formal as to be meaningless: 'What thou hast heard is something.' I insist I was not drunk, nor was I unable to imitate the sounds of English syllables. The stumbling-block was this: I could not permit an improper, ungrammatical string of words to pass my lips. I am an artist, after all.

The Americans shouted loud noises I could not understand. Then — I must have been standing too far forward — one of them spotted me. He pointed, yelled derisively, 'Hey! Al Jolson!' and hurled a brown beer bottle. It knocked over my clear bottle of gin; the alcohol streamed across my sandals. Another tossed bottle skittled my vermouth. The liquids mixed between my feet; the martini smell was overpowering. The Victrola, stuck in a groove, was repeating, 'How I love you . . . How I love you . . .' I was utterly shamed. I escaped from my recess, up the aisle (past the Usherette; her hair tickled my collarbone), through the swing doors, the lobby, the crossroads; caught a tram to the station and a train to Tokyo, where I still was, a month later, while the Superama cinema, White Crane Boulevard and most of Yokohama was being obliterated thrice in the course of six hours. The earthquake crumbled it, the fire burnt it, the tsunami swept it out to sea.

The only art I have left to me is the art of drinking and getting drunk. Each time, it is the same; each time, it is subtly different. Now, for instance, I am drinking a delicious martini cocktail. Actually, I am *not* drinking a delicious martini cocktail – gin and vermouth are unobtainable these days, because of the war – but saké. Everything tastes the same anyway.

Soon our noble army will land in California and destroy Hollywood. The 'talkie' will be outlawed. The art of the Speaker will be revived.

In the meantime, I converse with my beloved Usherette. 'I love thee for ever, my dearest,' I murmur to her. 'Nay, thou lovest me not, thou drunkard,' she replies. My head faces to the right; my head faces to the left.

A REAL COUNTRYWOMAN

Deborah Moggach

Deborah Moggach has published nine novels and adapted some for television. She has written a collection of short stories, *Smile*, and a stage-play, *Double Take*. She is now on her tenth novel and writing the screenplay of *The Stand-In*. She lives in London.

'A Real Countrywoman' was first broadcast on Radio 4, read by Elizabeth Mansfield.

We were sitting in the kitchen, opening Christmas cards. There was one from Sheila and Paul, whoever they were, and one from our bank manager, and one from my Aunty May which had been recycled from the year before. The last one was a brown envelope. Edwin opened it.

'My God!' he said. 'These bureaucrats have a piquant sense of timing.' He tugged at his beard – a newly-acquired mannerism. Since we had moved to the country he'd grown a beard; it made him look slightly like Jeremy Irons. Slightly.

The letter was from our County Council, and it said they were going to build a ring road right through our local wood.

Now, our local wood wasn't up to much but it was all we had. It was more a copse, really, across the field from our cottage. Like everything in the country it was surrounded by barbed wire, but I could worm my way through, with the children, and it was at least somewhere nearby to go. Such places are necessary, with small children.

It was full of brambles, and trees I couldn't name because I had always lived in London, and there was a small black pond which smelled like damp laundry. Not a lot grew in the wood, except Diet Pepsi cans. But I loved it, and now I knew it was condemned I appreciated its tangled rustlings, just as one listens more intently to a person who is going to die.

'A two-lane dual carriageway!' said Edwin. 'Right past our front door. Thundering pantechnicons!' This exploded from him like an oath. He went off to work, and every time the children broke something that morning, which was often, we cried 'Thundering pantechnicons!' But that wasn't going to keep them away.

Ours is a pretty, but not pretty enough to be protected, part of Somerset. People were going to campaign against this ring road, but the only alternative route was through our MP's daughter's riding school, so there wasn't much hope. That afternoon I drove off to look for holly. When you live in the country you spend your whole time in the car. This was our first Christmas in the country, the first of our new pure life, and I was trying to work up a festive spirit unaided by the crass high-street commercialism that Edwin was so relieved to escape. Me too, of course.

This time next Christmas, I thought, the thundering pantechnicons will be rattling our window-panes and filling our rooms with lead pollution. It will be just like Camden Town, all over again, but without the conversation.

That's what I missed, you see. Edwin didn't because he has inner resources. He's the only person I have ever met who has actually read *The Faerie Queene*. He has a spare, linear mind and fine features; nobody would ever, ever think of calling him Ed. When we lived in London, in Camden Town, he taught graphics. But then his art school was dissolved into another one and he lost his job. The government was brutish and philistine and London was full of fumes, so he said we should move to the country and I followed in the hot slipstream of his despair.

'Look at the roses growing in our children's cheeks!' he cried out, startling me, soon after we moved.

It was all right for him. He had people to talk to. He became a carpenter and he worked with three men, all of them bearded. They toiled in a barn, looking like an illustration in my old *Golden Book of Bible Stories*, while Fats Waller played on their cassette recorder.

Perhaps if I joined this anti-road campaign I could meet intelligent men like Jonathan Porritt. Perhaps they didn't all live in NW1.

Edwin thought this was febrile, but Edwin had inner resources. I only had the children. You can't have both.

And then, on Boxing Day, I had a brainwave.

It was freezing outside and the cat had had an accident in front of the Aga. Well, not an accident; she just hadn't bothered to go outside. Edwin was clearing it up with some newspaper when he stopped, and read a corner.

'Listen to this,' he said. 'The local council is spending

£19,000 on four underpasses, specially constructed for wildlife.'

At the time I wasn't really listening. I was throwing old roast potatoes into the hen bucket and working out how long it was since Edwin and I had made love.

'It's to save a colony of great crested newts,' he said.

We hadn't even on Christmas night, after some wonderful Australian Cabernet Sauvignon. The last time was Thursday week, when we had been agreeing how awful his mother was. This always drew us close. We had one or two such mild, but reliable, aphrodisiacs.

Then I thought about the campaign, and I suddenly caught up with what he had said about the newts.

It was such a simple idea, so breathtakingly simple, that my legs felt boneless and I had to sit down.

I didn't know much about natural history when all this happened, last Christmas. I was brought up in Swiss Cottage and spent my childhood with my nose pressed against shop windows, first toys then bikes then clothes.

Then Edwin and I married and we went to live in Camden Town. Streets were bedimmed with sulphuric emissions and we only recognised the changing seasons by the daffodil frieze at Sketchleys (Spring) and the Back-to-Skool promotion at Rymans (Autumn).

So I came to the country green, as it were. And after a year of organic gardening all I had learned was how to drive into Taunton, buy most of the stuff at Marks & Spencers and then pretend it was ours. It's so tiring, being organic. Being married, for that matter.

The day after Boxing Day I walked across to the wood, alone. It was a still, grey morning and without its foliage the place looked thin and vulnerable; I could see right through it. But now I knew what I was going to do, I felt possessive. I didn't own the wood, of course – it belonged to our local farmer, Mr Hodgkins, and he wanted the ring road because it meant he could retire to Portugal.

I got out my bin liners, and set to work. It's amazing, how much you can do when you don't have three children with you. In an hour I had tut-tutted my way through the place, filled three black bags and scratched my hands.

That evening I didn't watch TV. I looked through Edwin's library instead. He was in his potting shed, running off campaign leaflets on his printing press. Nursing my burning hands, I leafed through his *Complete British Wild Flowers*. I had no idea there were so many plants, and with such names – sneezewort and dodder, maids' bonnets and biting stonecrop. Poetic and unfamiliar, they danced in my head. I noted all the most endangered species. I hadn't learned so much since school.

When Edwin returned he was surprised I wasn't watching the TV. So was I.

'I want to learn more about the countryside,' I said.

He was terribly pleased. We started talking about his youth, in Dorset, where his father was a vicar. We talked about the years before graphics department politics, and children, and trying to find people rich enough to buy his tables.

'I wanted to be Edward Lear,' he said. 'To explore the world and find everything curious.'

'Wasn't he lonely?'

He nodded. 'But what an artist.' He paused, tugging his beard. 'Everybody has a time when they should have lived.'

'When's yours?' I asked.

'1890.'

'Think how much it would have hurt at the dentist's,' I said.

He laughed. 'When's yours?'

'Now.'

That night, despite our cold feet, we made love – the first time since that Thursday. He even kissed my ears, something I had forgotten I adored. He used to do it a lot in London.

Afterwards he said: 'I've been worried about you, Ruth. Have I been bossy?' I shook my head.

Mabel Cudlipp had newts. She was a fellow mother. I had seen her at the school gates for a year now, but we had never really talked. To tell the truth, I thought the mothers here looked boring compared to the London ones, who arrived at school breathing wine fumes from long lunches. Anyway, when the spring term began I started chatting, and it turned out that Mabel Cudlipp had some in her pond.

'Great crested newts,' she said. 'They're very rare. In fact, they've been protected since 1981.'

'You couldn't possibly spare one or two?'

She nodded. 'They're hibernating now, but we can look when it gets warmer.'

You might wonder why I didn't tell Edwin. The trouble was: his honesty. Once he drove twenty-two miles in freezing fog to pay somebody back when I had overcharged them for eggs. But that was when we were quarrelling, so you could call it marital politics.

Nor did I involve the children. Throughout that spring I worked away during school hours, accompanied only by Abbie, who is three and who couldn't sneak on me. She carried the trowel on our daily trips to the wood, which I now considered ours, its every clump of couch grass dear to me. When boxes arrived from obscure plant nurseries I told Edwin that I was really getting to grips with the garden. He was delighted, of course. While he battled against the bureaucrats – the Stop the Road campaign wasn't getting anywhere – I glowed, my cheeks grew roses, my fingernails were full of mud. I felt as heavy as a fruit with my secret; I hadn't felt so happy since I was pregnant.

I was also becoming something of an expert. For instance, on *Potamogeton densus* and *Riccia fluitans*. Latin names to you, but essential aquatic oxygenerators to me. I bought them at my local garden centre, which had an Ornamental Pond section, and carried them to the wood in plastic bags. I had dug out the pond, and turfed its sides.

Then there was *Triturus cristatus*, or perhaps *cristati* because there were four of them, courtesy of Mabel. Perhaps you don't know what this is. It is the great crested newt. The male has a silver streak on the tail, and at breeding-time develops a high, crinkled crest and a bright orange belly. The female, without crest but with skin-flap above and below tail, is slightly longer than the male. *I* was feeling slightly longer than the male; more vigorous and powerful.

For good measure, and why not, Abbie and I planted some surprising plants in the wood too, garden plants and some blue Himalayan poppies. I had to use my credit card for most of this, the whole operation was costing a fortune. And there were the orchids. We planted the lady's-slipper, the lizard and the bird's-nest, all extremely rare and purchased from a small nursery in Suffolk whose address I had found in the back of *Amateur Gardener*. I cut off all the labels, of course, I'm not a complete fool, I even went to university once. I planted them tenderly in the patches I had cleared amongst the brambles. Above us the birds sang, and the watery spring sunshine gleamed on the ivy which, lush as leather, trousered the trees. I even knew the trees' names now.

In all those weeks Edwin never visited the wood. He never had time. In the country people never have time to do things like that, unless someone comes to lunch. It's like living in London and never visiting the Tate Gallery until some American friends arrive. Edwin was busy doing all the things that people who live in the country really do, like driving twenty miles to collect the repaired lawnmower, and then doing it all over again because the lawnmower still didn't work. So he never knew.

Well, they didn't build the ring road past us, they're building it through the riding stables. This is because our wood has been designated a site of outstanding scientific interest. They've put up a proper wooden fence, and a sign. They're even thinking of building a car-park. And instead of thundering pantechnicons we've now got thundering Renaults full of newt-watchers.

It's Boxing Day today and people have come from all over, it's been really interesting. They knock on our door, and ask the way, and admire our cottage – botanists in particular are very polite. We're doing a brisk trade in eggs, too. Ours are guaranteed salmonella-free because the hens are fed on my organic bread; which is so disgusting that we're always throwing it away. Sometimes the people even leave their children here, to play with mine, while they tramp across the field to look at the orchids. Danny, that's my eldest, has even started saying things like 'mega-crucial', and now we have our own traffic jams I don't miss Camden Town at all.

What Edwin feels about this is best described as mixed. Still, his furniture business is booming because it's only two miles away and even he is materialistic enough to have put up a notice, with a sepia photograph and a map, pointing them in the right direction. And so much has happened during the day that we don't have to talk about his mother any more.

When spring comes, and the flowers start blooming, I've decided to start doing teas. I'll buy Old-Style Spiced Buns at Marks and Sparks and throw away the packets.

I've learned a lot this past year, you see. About the *real* country way of doing things.

SOMETHING OF FANCY

A. L. Barker

A. L. Barker left school at sixteen and after the war joined the BBC. Her debut collection of stories, *Innocents*, won the first Somerset Maugham Prize in 1947 and her novel *John Brown's Body* was short-listed for the Booker Prize in 1969. Her last short-story collection was *Any Excuse for a Party* and she is at present working on another novel.

'Something of Fancy' was first broadcast on Radio 4, read by Joanna Myers and Clarence Smith.

I am in the habit of sitting here where I have a tolerable view of the Cathedral, one of the few things unchanged. The birds are as they always were, thrushes, starlings – impudent and noisy – and tiny wrens fluttering their wings in nervous haste. I fancy the sky is not the same: it is heavier and smaller, quite cramped, in fact.

But that is an absurd conceit. On reflection I realise that it is due to the preponderance of tall buildings and, no doubt, to my having passed much of my time in country places, though the trees do not seem so lofty as when I watched them stirring in the wind like proud argosies with spreading sails and straining timbers.

This increase in my sensibilities affords me no pleasure. I am conscious of being quite alone. While my own company has never been a burden to me, indeed it has often been most necessary and I have the best recollections of it, this is a new experience: of alienation rather than solitude. And so very chilly.

Even the fall in temperature is exceptional, it seems to influence not me but my immediate surroundings and I have the distinct impression that it goes far beyond these. How to describe it? I still feel the compulsion to note it down. It is as if our planet has removed to another quarter of the universe, leaving me with my precepts and persuasions intact. I sit here in the expectation of something which will change *me*.

Every day a young man comes and walks to and fro on the grass where walking is strictly prohibited. His clothes evidence wear and somewhat judicial tear, as for effect rather than usage. Since he arrives always at noon I have supposed him to be a student escaping from his books for a little air and exercise.

His person is unprepossessing: he wears his hair tied in a knot, has an ill-disposed countenance of irregular features unredeemed by a large gold ring in one ear. He gestures constantly, holding up his arms to heaven and occasionally falling to his knees, blaspheming or beseeching I cannot tell which. I think it is something of each.

Passers-by shun him, mothers draw their children away, old people avert their eyes. Well they may, he has a wild and sullen look which now he bends on me.

One day he came to where I sit. It was mizzling with rain but he threw himself down beside me with such a reckless disregard that the wooden bench rocked.

'Think I don't know what you're thinking?' His tone was offensive. I replied coldly that I hadn't considered it.

'Not worth it, eh?'

I said that since I did not know him, my thought could only be hypothetical.

'I've seen you watching me. I can read you – a, b, c, it's as easy as that. This guy's a phoney, a weirdo, a wino, chasing the tiger – that's what you think.'

I think he habitually neglects his toilet, a sad portent for himself and a discourtesy to the world in general.

'You think I'm a hophead because I have big, big feelings, bigger than myself.' He leaned close to look into my face. I shall not say he is a stranger to soap and water, but certainly he has not washed so recently as common hygiene requires. 'Don't know what I'm talking about, do you? No matter. I've got to talk this thing through. I've tried talking it to no one, I tried talking it to Sam Beckett, I've got his picture in my room. But you're someone, and I don't give a toss whether you listen or not so long as you sit here while I talk.'

I said I was prepared to listen. I am still hoping to hear something to my advantage. Though I want for nothing, I feel a curious lack. It is perhaps that very want I feel the lack of.

But he fell silent, stretching out his legs to the peril of passers-by and gazing at a device tattooed on his forearm, a serpent entwining a tree. I wondered if he was not a student but a sailor, it being the fashion among seafaring men to ornament themselves thus.

After a few moments' contemplation, during which he

flexed and unflexed the muscles of his arm, causing the serpent to appear to move round the tree, he turned and addressed himself to me with the words: 'Do you believe in sex without marriage?'

I no longer blush, I am denied that ephemeral warmth. But the question came as a profound surprise. I kept my composure and made reply that I considered a happy marriage the best fate for everyone. It is a fate I once had high hopes of for myself.

At the same time I felt I was living a dream. The world receded, I did not miss it, for I was not alone as I am now. Sweet tenderness and purest passion were promised me. During those few brief days I looked into my heart and saw true happiness in store. Even the necessary parting did not threaten it, for we had the most reliable expectations of meeting again. But instead there came that other last encounter which must come, timely or untimely, to us all. We never saw each other again.

'Okay,' said the young man, 'I knew you wouldn't.'

I understood, I said, that gentlemen had special requirements and I believed that for financial considerations these could be met.

'Are you codding me?' He it was who coloured, a dark and angry crimson. 'If you are, I'm here to tell you I don't take that from anyone. I asked a straight question, I want a straight answer.'

I protested that I intended no mockery, we were of different generations and a straight answer in his was an impropriety in mine.

'You're not that old. About the same age as my mother. She uses three-letter words all the time.'

Since I was not certain if this made her commendable, I remained silent.

'Listen, I'll put it to you straight. There's him and this girl – his name's Hugh but everyone calls him Huge because he is. Basically he's a sweet guy, she's a chanteuse and stripper in the local disco. They've been together for weeks and it looked like being a good relationship, but she won't get into bed. Now that's serious, he's taken up modelling for art classes in the evenings to make ends meet and she's upsetting his concentration, he can't hold his poses, he has trouble with himself but he won't try group therapy. Cassandra can't see his problem –' He looked at me. 'What's up?'

I had to tell him that Cassandra was my sister's name.

'Okay. There was this ancient Greek woman who kept opening her mouth and putting her foot in it, that's why I chose the name. It's relevant, see. I'm a novelist, I'm writing a book about sexual anarchy.'

I said that in the widest sense it must be the theme, or contributory theme, of every novel ever written.

'Not the way I'm going to do it. I'm dealing with basic emotions, human sacrifices, voodoo, deep-down animal instincts, ape-men hunting in primeval forests – where it all started.'

Who has not wondered at the hair's-breadth between ignoble savage and our civilised society? I have had occasion to wonder in parlours and drawing rooms, at elegant suppers, whilst drinking tea with ladies of breeding and reputation.

'It's going to be deep, red-blooded stuff, not for Festival of Literature types.'

At this point I felt constrained to say that such conception as we can have of primitive peoples is necessarily limited, for we cannot fully conceive of their brutish lives and poverty of spirit. I said I believed that such details as we choose to guess at should be presented in manner suited to the degree of refinement we have now achieved.

'This thing that's holding her back is bigger than she is. Know what I mean?'

Is her virtue, I thought, still all a woman has to lose?

'I'm going to have her come right out and declare herself in front of everyone. Sort of a manifesto, it will be one of the big moments in the book.'

It would certainly be dramatic, I said, but would it not manifest only a private conviction which would be better hid?

'Are you telling me how to write this book?'

I said I would not presume, but it had been my experience,

in life and in fiction, that this particular conviction was readily disposed of when sufficient pressure was brought to bear.

'You don't say.'

He was plainly not willing to take advice from me, but I have never been able to resist proffering it. It was generally accepted, I pointed out, that men were destined to subjugate women, that they were equipped by Nature to do so. According to popular superstition a man, any man, was superior to any woman. He was an enigma, and a rarity, although in fact the members of his sex might outnumber ours two to one. It appeared that this concept still prevailed, though I had hoped it would by now have been discredited.

'Like I said, this book's deep. I'm into resonances and sympathetic vibrations, I'm fully hooked up, I *connect*. Know what I mean?'

I knew, and should thank him for it. From what strange source may come our help!

'The book's all done but for the ending. That's got to come over big, hit the reader between the eyes.'

Perhaps he should pause to consider, I said, that seldom, very seldom, did complete truth belong to any human disclosure. Seldom could it happen that something was not a little disguised or a little mistaken.

He held up his index and second fingers in a gesture unfamiliar to me but intended, I was sure, to be derisory.

'The way I spell it out there won't be any mistake. It will be the only really red-blooded novel to win the Booker, put twenty thousand pounds in my pocket, guarantee my sales and get me an advance of a hundred thousand for my next.'

Though I was sorry that he should give way to such wild imaginings, politeness was – could only be – my response. I had written a little myself, I said, and understood his concern.

'You?' His smile scarcely improves him. 'What sort of thing do you write?'

Something of fancy, I said, and something of imagination.

The rain was now persistent. How it would have vexed me had I been wearing my hat with the silken flowers! This young man's clothes smelled like wet animal's fur. The trees above us began to drip steadily into our laps.

And then something — the gentle function of the rain on the leaves perhaps — brought back to me most poignant memories of my home in the midst of meadows, elm and chestnut trees, with here and there a darker presence of firs. I recalled the strawberry beds in my father's garden, the lanes decked with violets and primroses in spring. In that dear landscape was surely one of the joys of heaven.

And the old house, so plain and pleasant, whitewashed walls reflecting the light of day and the glow of candles by night — there I spent so many happy hours of childhood.

My writings, I said, would not bear comparison with his spirited prose.

He was not listening, he rounded on me, crying, 'I've got it — my ending! Listen — Cassandra's there on stage, in the middle of her number, she's singing about love and death. She pulls a knife and stabs Huge. They all see her do it. Someone starts on the bongo drums and it turns into a ritual kill. The drumbeat sends them crazy, they start ripping each other up and the book ends with them all dead except Cass — and what do you know? This is the punch-line — she's the only one who doesn't want to live.' He glowed with rain and inspiration. 'How's that for size?'

I said it was very comprehensive, but took warning when his face began to darken and added that I thought it significant — which I might fairly do without specifying what it signified.

'I tell you it's colossal! Megatonic!'

As he appeared to be well satisfied and not in want of further encouragement and was getting wetter in his person than could be good for his health, I stood up, prepared to take my departure.

He would have seized me by the shoulders had I not drawn back, putting a sufficient distance of grass between us. I hoped, I said, that his book would be well received and financially successful.

'Wait — where are you going?'

To College Street, I said. It had become clear to me that it is from there I must begin my journey to the place reserved for me.

'Hi – what's your name?'

I did not wait. I said he would find my name in College Street.

There exists a plaque on the wall of No. 8, stating that Jane Austen lived her last days in that house and died on 18 July 1817.

LIFE WITHOUT GEORGE

Lynne Truss

Lynne Truss used to be Literary Editor of *The Listener* and is now television critic for *The Times*. She is currently writing a novel.

'Life Without George' was first broadcast on Radio 4, read by Michael Williams.

It was Christmas morning, and the Baileys' house on the upper Thames stood like a cake decoration on a thin layer of freshly fallen snow. As I approached the house, it seemed to me that every window glared with yellow light, shutting out the cold and darkness. I stood in the neglected garden and by the large picture window of the sitting room I paused, unseen, to stare in at George: he and his four revolting children, relaxing after the morning's rippings and shoutings, lay about in loose pyjamas, turning all their open-mouthed attention to the inanities of Christmas morning television. That's him, I thought, that's George: you will live to know me better.

I carried on around the house, leaving no footprint, casting no shadow. In the dining room, I saw the table was already laid with crystal glasses and festive serviettes, and the sideboard sported ugly doilies and plastic litres of fizzy coloured drinks. At last I reached the steamed-up window of the kitchen, which a silhouette of a woman was struggling to open. That's her, I thought, that's Mary. As she flung the window wide and stuck out her head for breath, I looked her full in the face. You are not a happy woman, I said, but she didn't hear me, of course. Stars twinkled and pulsed in the still-dark morning sky. They might have been talking to one another.

That will be Harry, I thought, looking along the road. A taxi was just about to come into view, its headlights scanning the hedgerows, its suspension banging when the driver took the humpbacked bridge too fast. Harry was sitting in the back, nervously counting his parcels for the fifth time, and tilting his watch to catch some light. He had never liked this bridge – he fell off it as a child, and had to be 'rescued' from the river by George, who never let him forget it. George had become a bit of a hero; Harry had got the reputation of being a wimp, which had dogged his life. He swallowed a tot of whisky from his hip-flask, and tried to listen to what the taxi-driver was saying.

'He a friend of yours, this Mr Bailey?' asked the taxi-driver.

'No. I mean, yes. He's my brother.'

'Tell him I've had my house repossessed, will you? Make his Christmas, I bet. He's the bloke from the building society, right? He got me a hundred per cent mortgage last year, on a £75,000-house, and I can't pay it any more. They took away my house. The wife's gone off, and the kids have just gone into care.'

'I don't know —'

'All right. Here we are. That's twenty-six quid. Double fare Christmas.'

I saw the taxi drive off. Harry was left standing on the snowy gravel, with an empty wallet and a small pile of parcels on the ground beside him. Through the window he could see the scene on the television — a star of *Hi-De-Hi!* was bearing down with gruesome intent on sick children in a hospital ward. He rang the bell, and watched as George, predictably, made no effort to get up. He rang again — even the children didn't react, but he saw the outline of his sister-in-law appear through the frosted glass, and then fiddle with the lock.

'Harry!' She looked flustered but pleased to see him. She was holding a rasher of bacon; and there was gravy powder in her hair.

'Just trying to get the dinner ready. Come in.'

The phone rang, and she rushed to answer it, distractedly pushing the bacon at Harry as she passed. 'Hello? Violet . . . Of course you must come here. What has he done now? . . . oh . . . oh dear . . . oh . . . Look, just come over, I must get on with the dinner. But you're very welcome.'

George appeared at the hall door, his body facing his brother, but his eyes fixed on the television. 'You'd better come in,' he said.

'That was Violet, dear,' said Mary. 'Violet Bicks. That friend of yours has been beating her up again. I sometimes think you shouldn't have tried to help her at all. Anyway, she's coming over.' Mary closed the kitchen door behind her.

'Get yourself a drink,' said George. He didn't want to hear about Violet: he'd only helped her to get her out of his hair. He slumped back down in his chair. *The Snowman* was on now, which he never liked very much; but the day was growing lighter, so soon the telly people would be going 'live' to a crowd of people in padded coats and moonboots in a field somewhere. They did that every Christmas and he never missed it. He liked to see the damn fools waving at the cameras.

'Taxi-driver said he'd lost his house.'

'Ernie was it? Stupid bugger. Shouldn't have taken it on if he couldn't pay it. He's not the only one, though; we've had loads of people overstretch themselves. This bit with the flying is all right.'

'What?'

'*The Snowman.*'

'Oh. Actually, I lost my job again, George.'

'What, Sainsbury's?'

'No, that was before. The Texaco.'

'Sorry about that, Harry. He is cute, though, isn't he? I think I've got a scarf like that somewhere.'

'I think I might be heading for another nervous breakdown, George.'

'That Keith Chegwin will be on in a minute.'

In the kitchen I saw Mary survey the sea of ghastliness. The turkey wasn't cooking fast enough, the roast potatoes had got ahead of themselves and were dark, tough and shiny, like Bakelite. A rasher of bacon had mysteriously found its way on to a light fitting in the hall. She had left the brandy butter open on a shelf, and the cats had eaten half of it before she noticed. One of the kids ran through, and knocked her elbow just as she was raising a valium to her lips: now she was shaking. The dinner had to be over by half past two, so that George could watch *It's a Wonderful Life* again.

She tried to remember what happens in the first hour or so, since she would be washing up during that part. But all she could remember was the second half, where James Stewart is

shown by an angel what would have happened in the world
– how ghastly it would have been – if he had never been
born. His wife would have been an old maid; his brother
would have died; his childhood sweetheart would have
turned to prostitution; people wouldn't have been able to
buy their own houses. It made her cry every time. It seemed
right for Christmas – to think about how much better things
were than they might have been. She spotted the valium on
top of a mince pie. 'Thank you God,' she said aloud, and had
swallowed it before you could say 'Frank Capra'.

I ought to say that *It's a Wonderful Life* always makes me
cry too. Everything works out so perfectly. I've been trying
for 250 years to get things to work out as well as that. So I
was glad when dinner was over, and I could make my move.
George was settling back into his chair; the lights were off.
He unbuttoned his trousers with a wink to Harry and
grabbed the remote control as *It's a Wonderful Life* began.

'I thought this was in colour?'

'No. I don't think so.'

'They ought to turn them all into colour. That's what I pay
my licence for. They can do it now, you know.'

As the warmth and the dinner dragged George's spirit deep
into the comfy chair, I stepped through the wall, making the
Christmas tinsels dance and sparkle in the silvery light from
the screen. I tugged his sleeve, and all at once we were standing side by side in a bitter wind atop the humpbacked
bridge. George opened his eyes and howled, 'What the –' and
slipped from my grasp back into the cosy living room. I strode
in again, and pulled him from the chair, and once again we
stood out in the cold, me in my eighteenth-century dress, he
in his Christmas-present cardigan and slippers. It is a good
effect at any time, but I heightened it: whereas the scene in
the house had been in colour, we were now in black and
white.

'Who are you?' asked George. 'What's going on?'

'I am your guardian angel. I came because I sensed despair

in you, George Bailey,' I said (I had been briefed to say this).
'I thought you might be thinking of killing yourself.'

'Why would I want to do that?' demanded George. 'My
life is great, wonderful. Let me go home, it's freezing. And
where's the colour gone from this cardigan?' He looked at
his arms in disbelief. 'It was green: Mary gave it to me. I
didn't like it very much but at least it wasn't grey.'

'I'm sorry, George, but I've had my orders. I have come to
show you what would have happened if you had never been
born.'

'Listen, you dunderhead: I wasn't thinking of killing
myself. That's in the film. Everything is fine – you don't have
to convince me of anything. Can I go home now please?'

But I have been trained in obstinacy, so although I said,
'Very well, we can go home now,' I deliberately led him back
to a slightly different house, with a much nicer garden.

'What's happened? Whose car is that? Why are the curtains
closed? What's happened in the garden? Where the hell is my
satellite dish?' I was jolly pleased by all this: George thrashed
around in a rare confusion. It was really very gratifying.

'It's someone else's house now, George. Someone who
looks after the garden, evidently. It's because you were never
born. Do you believe me now? Do you see? Look, there's
Ernie the taxi-man: let's go into town and see what we can
see.'

George reacted. 'Not Ernie, no. He hates me. I got him a
mortgage that he couldn't keep up.'

'That won't matter now, you'll see,' I said, rather smugly.
(Angels are allowed to be a bit smug sometimes.)

I hailed the taxi and we got in.

'Why are you working on Christmas Day, my friend?' I
asked – though George was signalling to me to shut up. 'Do
you need the money so very much?'

'No,' laughed Ernie – who seemed quite a different fellow
now. 'I've never got out of my depth finance-wise, though I
had a narrow escape last year. I was thinking about a big
mortgage, but luckily a kind man at the building society
explained all the risks. No, my family is planning a big lovely

warm-hearted Christmassy surprise for me at home, so I said I'd go out for a while. I didn't expect to see anyone else, tell you the truth.'

We travelled on into town, George staring out of the window at the grey scene. The shopfronts on the High Street were disappointingly unaltered by his state of not-having-been-born. The building society was just the same as ever. Everything was closed and dark anyway, except the library, which was brightly lit. As we passed, we saw that inside a young woman was standing on a small stepladder, adjusting a painting on the wall.

'Stop!' shouted George. 'There's Mary. Look.' And so it was – though it looked like a prettier and a younger Mary. I had to look at my watch to check we hadn't slipped back in time. George flung open the door and scrambled over the snow in his slippers, to get a closer look. I thanked Ernie ('No charge. Merry Christmas!') and joined George. Mary didn't see us, but we watched her for a full half-hour. She moved gracefully and confidently, adjusting pictures and stopping occasionally to smile at some private joke, or take a sip from an elegant wineglass. MARY HATCH RETROSPEC-TIVE, said the sign on an easel in the window, OPENS BOXING DAY.

I must say I was beginning to feel a bit sorry for George. He was looking crestfallen, as well he might. For one thing, his slippers were getting completely ruined.

'What's this supposed to prove?' he asked, sulkily.

He had me there. I was beginning to wonder myself.

'Look, cheer up,' I said. 'There's obviously some mistake. I mean, *all right*: Mary would have been happier perhaps if you had never been born. Okay, we'll concede that. I mean, well, possibly even lots happier. But you've done all sorts of good things in your life: you saved Harry, you rescued Violet from a fate worse than death. Let's not forget those things.'

George brightened a little. 'Are you going to take me to the cemetery, to show me Harry's gravestone?'

'Yes, I am. This way, I think.' And we struck out for the church.

It was about three-thirty, and the bells were ringing for evensong as we arrived at the church gates. In the porch a little crowd had gathered, and we waved at the vicar as we dodged around the church to the graveyard.

'You go that way,' shouted George. 'There's not much light left.' And he started frantically pulling overgrown grass away from a headstone.

'I have a torch,' said a voice, from behind a Victorian tomb.

'Who said that?' asked George, still pulling.

'May I help you? Who are you looking for?'

'Harry Bailey,' snapped back George.

'How extraordinary,' said the figure, stepping into view, and shining the torch into his own face. '*My* name is Harry Bailey.'

It was the vicar. And it was Harry. George fainted.

George regained consciousness in the vestry, and came face to face with a brother he never had. Harry, like Mary, looked younger and sweeter. I wondered if I should slip out for a minute and call back to base: perhaps I should abandon this operation altogether. George took it rather well, I thought, the story Harry told us about how he nearly drowned as a child, and how he had heard the voice of God calling to him. His brush with death had made him a stronger person, he was sure. He asked whether we needed spiritual guidance, and I said no I didn't, but perhaps George could do with some.

The wind rattled the vestry door, and George began to sob. This was terrible. As a last resort, I thought I'd better raise the subject of Violet Bicks – did Harry know her? He sprang to his feet. 'Violet Bicks? Are you from the press?' I said I didn't understand.

'Ever since that court case about the luncheon vouchers in Streatham, Violet has been a household name. And she keeps coming back here to show off all the money she's made from her book and film. She is still a dear friend, of course, but I do find her very embarrassing. I wouldn't be surprised if that wasn't her arriving right now.'

And sure enough, George's last chance of redemption swept past us in a fur coat, waving and blowing kisses over her shoulder amid a volley of flash guns.

George fainted again.

Back at the house, the body of George was tossing about on the chair. He looked contented, but I knew he was lost in the agony of a dream. Perhaps I should just bring him home now: it seemed unlikely I was going to 'get my wings' with this one. I looked around the house: in the kitchen, Mary was crying over a sink full of greasy water; she had just tried to unblock the S-bend with a plunger, and her dress and face were dirty and wet. Harry sat drinking in a chair by the fire, casting a fuddled glance at George every so often, not sure which would make George more angry – to be woken up, or not to be woken up. Violet had just arrived and was in the downstairs bathroom, trying to cover up a black eye with a cheap cream foundation. On the telly, James Stewart had just decided that he would rather have been alive, and was running back to his house and family, shouting 'Merry Christmas' to everyone in Bedford Falls.

I led George back from town, and we stopped on the bridge. He was crying, and I couldn't think of a sensible way of consoling him. What could I tell him that would make things seem better? I tried to get help ('Joseph, help me'), but all the lines seemed to be busy. You know what it's like on Christmas Day. So in the end, I thought: why not do what the angel did in the film? I could jump into the river, and he could save me. Surely that would make him feel worth while? Two splashes and a life saved after all. I realise now that it wasn't the best idea in the world: but, as I said later at the heavenly tribunal, how was I to know about his dicky heart?

When the film came to an end, the whole household was gathered around the television to shed a few tears. Mary had come in from the kitchen with a tray of tea. Harry and Violet, each the worse for a few drinks, were shaking with emotion. In the film, a little bell rang on James Stewart's Christmas tree, and everybody laughed because it meant the angel had got his wings for saving a man's life. I wondered how many millennia it was going to take before I got mine.

I looked at George, but he didn't stir. I tugged his sleeve but I knew it was no good. He wasn't going to wake up. Way downstream, in the frozen afternoon, George was floating in the moonlight.

THE PUNISHMENT OF LUXURY

Michael Carson

Michael Carson was born in Merseyside and has worked in various countries including Saudi Arabia, Brunei and Iran. He has contributed over twenty stories to BBC Radio and has published four novels. He is now working on number five and continues to write for *Short Story* on Radio 4.

'The Punishment of Luxury' was first broadcast on Radio 4, read by Bob Peck.

The Dark Green government demanded that extensive coverage be given to the first execution of a citizen convicted under the new Transportation Act. Broadcasting equipment was brought to Trafalgar Square by bicycle, tricycle and solar-powered scooter, and set up around Vehicle Compacter No. 1, to the south of Sperm Whale column.

A crowd gathered from early morning. Around eight, six Dark Green Ecological Enforcers pushed a black Jaguar into the Square. Its owner, the condemned man, Dr Robert Stone of Cattawade, Essex, had been arrested, tried, convicted, and was now about to be executed for being found in possession of an automobile. This crime would have been sufficient to ensure that the doctor spent the rest of his natural life in uncomfortably natural surroundings, but what had brought down the full rigours of the new law upon his head was that he had actually been caught *driving* his car.

The unfortunate Dr Stone had been spotted indulging in this unnatural practice by a Dark Green Reformer while reforming ex-driving instructors on a piece of forestry land adjacent to the doctor's property. He had been trekking with his charges through this wilderness, pointing out the ravages wrought by acid rain on the trees. The disgraced prisoners – many in tears, their ancient car-coats hanging in tatters from their wasted frames – were kissing the trunks of damaged trees reverently, begging forgiveness of the Wisdom and Spirit of the Universe as they did so. The Dark Green Reformer had been about to sing a verse of his favourite song, 'A Tree is Worth a Hundred People', when he had smelled something unpleasant. 'Surely not . . .' he thought and launched into the first verse:

> 'A tree is worth a hundred people
> A flower a thousand hammers
> A compost heap is . . .'

203

But then he stopped and sniffed again. He looked up into the trees where baby cuckoos were throwing baby blackbirds out of nests as Nature intended. He inhaled again. The smell took him back more than a decade, and he saw himself riding through Central London in the gutter on his old Raleigh, looking out for glass, cursing the cars, smelling that smell. Then he saw the old Jaguar, with Dr Stone sitting furtively behind the wheel, moving along the drive nearby.

The Dark Green Reformer and his band of traffic criminals gasped. Dr Stone had been arrested and brought in chains to the Old Bailey in a police rickshaw.

The Jaguar was placed next to the compacter. The doctor sat stoically as the Ecological Enforcers pushed the vehicle into the machine. The public executioner flicked the switch. The compacter rumbled into life. The peace of rush-hour London was shattered. Goat-hands had trouble controlling their herds on the Whitehall allotments. Shire ponies shied. Thousands of pigeons, unused to a mechanical sound, took to the air in panic, wheeling and flapping. Even the ripening wheat in Kensington Gardens seemed to tremble. The doomed doctor looked up and caught sight of the steeple of St Martin's with birds soaring all around it. Then he saw the passenger door to his left coming towards him, the roof of the car crumple, approaching and retreating.

Five minutes later, the compacter opened its jaws to reveal a solid black-and-grey cube. This was manhandled to a corner of Trafalgar Square and placed on a plinth directly opposite the National Gallery of Batik. A sign was placed below the compacted Jaguar-and-Doctor Stone which read:

THE PUNISHMENT OF LUXURY

That evening Arnold Watney watched news of the execution on his solar-powered green-and-grey television in Wolverhampton, set up on the street between the Jolly Miller Fruit Juice Pub and the Rude Health You-Bag-It Store. As he watched, he shook, thinking of Mabel the Morris Minor hidden under a sheet in his lounge at home. The crowd watching the television around him cheered and whooped as the compacter began its work. The cameras strafed the crowd. To the accompaniment of 'Ode to Joy', children with perfect teeth waved Dark Green flags and chewed on NuttiFroot bars; housewives in handloom clothing shouted abuse at the sorely-pressed doctor, saying that crushing was too good for him.

Arnold Watney, feeling guilty, tried to smell himself. He hoped that the peppermint leaves he had been chewing for the last half-hour would disguise the tobacco, the home-brew beer and the car-wax – any one of which would merit a serious charge against him.

Under the Greens, the nose had become an instrument of great sensitivity. No longer anaesthetised by tobacco, car fumes, solvents, and alcohol, it had won out over the eyes and ears of the State and was able to sniff out all manner of iniquity.

Arnold Watney fled from his compatriots, wondering what he should do. He wandered into the Freedom Allotments which covered the whole of what had until recently been the industrial area of Wolverhampton. He walked down the manicured paths kept shipshape by men with 'CONVICTED SMOKER' printed on their uniforms. He walked past the Rottweiler Sanctuary, then through the Arborarium. He could hear the chirping of birds but behind that sound, apart from the barking of Rottweilers, nothing but nothing disturbed the peace. Depression covered him like an illegal fishing-net.

Not for the first time he felt a deep desire ache through him to close the curtains in his lounge, uncover Mabel the Morris Minor, sit behind her leather-covered steering-wheel, light a cigarette and pretend to drive her, whispering 'Vruuum! Vruuum!' between his teeth. But that was not possible. That would never be possible again. Why, oh why, he wondered, hadn't he got rid of all the incriminating things in his life when it had been easy? But he knew why. He had been hoping the Dark Green party would be beaten in the election and the Light Greens returned. The Light Green administration in retrospect seemed like halcyon days to him now. They had tolerated the use of cars one day a week, providing one had four passengers, a valid reason for the journey, and one's itinerary plotted and submitted in triplicate on recycled paper. They allowed one to smoke herbal mixture. It was even to be bought – though at a considerable price – at the larger branches of Rude Health You-Bag-It stores nationwide. But the Dark Greens had cancelled elections until the world was once again clean. And cleanliness meant the eradication of dirty freedoms. Arnold Watney's panic rose. He was a dead man. At any moment the full weight of the Dark Green Revolutionary Cadre could sweep down on his house and take him away to share poor, crushed Dr Stone's fate.

His only hope, he felt, was to confess his wicked addictions to the Dark Green Cell at the Tofunutri Processing Cooperative, his place of employment. They might send him off for weekend re-education, or, if they thought his case severe enough, give him a sabbatical for the full treatment at the Dark Green Re-education Centre in Mid-Wales. He shuddered: he had heard tales of what happened there. One had to dust the leaves of trees day after day, clean out badger sets, nurse cows in the Mad Cow Home, all the time reciting apologetic mantras to Mother Nature.

But even to embark on this dire course of action he would have to rid himself of Mabel the Morris Minor, the home-brew buckets, the tobacco plants, everything that made his pathetic single life worth living.

Might it not be better, then, to die?

In bed that night Arnold Watney tossed and turned. He had more or less decided that life had to be better than the alternative, but the idea of parting with Mabel filled him with sadness, a sadness he was not sure he would ever recover from. Perhaps he would get over his addiction to tobacco and home-brew, but Mabel was his life.

Still, at half past one in the morning he got up and went downstairs. By candlelight he began to take Mabel the Morris Minor to bits, weeping with every turn of the wrench.

It took him the best part of a fortnight to trundle small sections of Mabel out of his house at dead of night on the trolley pulled by his bicycle. He rode bits of his wicked but wonderful Morris Minor silently down the lane and dumped her with some ceremony into an ornamental lilypond. Each night he was certain that he would be caught by someone, but somehow his luck held. On the last night he took his home-brew buckets and added them to the pyre in the pond.

At last he was clean! Let the Dark Greens search high and low! They wouldn't find anything to pin on him!

His heart, however, longed for Mabel. His lungs for a cigarette. His liver for a long cool pint of home-brew mild.

Arnold Watney confessed his deep cravings for uncleanliness to the Dark Green Cell at work. They shook their heads of herb-scented hair, and decided that he needed the full treatment. Arnold Watney joined a convoy of bicycles heading for Mid-Wales and the Re-education Centre.

He'd been dusting leaves, hugging trees and confessing his crimes to groups of fellow polluters for three weeks when news of the coup d'état reached them. The Dark Greens had been overthrown by a united coalition of Light Greens, Lilacs and The Pink Negative Population Party. Changes were being made. They were free!

He pedalled like mad back to Wolverhampton. Near Pembridge, Herefordshire, he passed some people digging up an old Volkswagen. In Warwick he saw a man with a fishing-rod, wearing an accursed Walkman. When he arrived in Wolverhampton his neighbours, as cool as cress, as bold as broccoli, were polishing their Ford Fiesta.

'I thought you'd got rid of that!' shouted a puffing Arnold Watney.

'We couldn't! We just couldn't!' confessed his neighbour, pulling on what looked suspiciously like a cigarette.

'Mabel! You've got to help me retrieve Mabel!' shouted the unreformed Arnold Watney.

An hour later, with the help of the neighbourhood, Arnold Watney was fishing Mabel the Morris Minor out of the lily-pond. Things would be easier from now on. The green-and-grey televisions spoke of *glasnost* and *perestroika*. Words such as compromise and step-by-step fell on the nation's ears like the igniting of a match, or an engine, or the first tender pangs of desire. Arnold Watney gazed lovingly at the pieces of wet car as they emerged one by one from the pure water. He bowed down and kissed Mabel's bonnet, wiped the tears away from her back axle. And he knew that as he toiled to put Mabel back together again his life too would get back on the right road.

But the coup had only been a clever Dark Green government ploy to flush out cars and other hated objects from their hiding-places, hypocrites from the concealed whited sepulchres of their desires. Two weeks later The Terror began in earnest. Up and down the country compacters crushed opposition without ceasing. And the Good Earth heaved a sigh of satisfaction on seeing Humankind put firmly – at long last – in its place.

CIRCLE OF FRIENDS

MAEVE BINCHY

'Binchy's novels are never less than entertaining, they are, without exception repositories of common sense and good humour, chronicled with tenderness and wit'
The Sunday Times

An enchanting novel of fierce loyalty and love in changing times.

Big generous-hearted Benny and the elfin Eve Malone have been best friends throughout their childhoods in sleepy Knockglen. When they both go to study in Dublin, they meet a circle of friends that includes handsome Jack Foley and the selfish but beautiful Nan Mahon – whose ambitions will drag them all into trouble.

As Knockglen is surprised into new life the two girls, Benny and Eve discover that among the many distractions of growing up true friendship is the greatest gift of all.

Post·A·Book

A Royal Mail service in association with the Book Marketing Council & The Booksellers Association.
Post-A-Book is a Post Office trademark.

VICTORIA LINE, CENTRAL LINE

MAEVE BINCHY

From Seven Sisters to Stockwell, from Shepherd's Bush to Chancery Lane, everyday life is never as dull as it might seem:

At Oxford Street two former rivals plot a murder; at Bond Street a shoplifter avoids the sales assistant's eye; at Tottenham Hale Amy worries about her domineering sister-in-law . . .

With characteristic humour and originality, Maeve Binchy has exposed an enthralling, wonderfully realistic cross-section of London life.

'Reading these tales is like listening to someone talking: someone you very much want to hear'
Sunday Telegraph

'Rare delights from an inveterate storyteller'
New Society

VICTORIA LINE and CENTRAL LINE were previously published as two separate volumes.

HODDER AND STOUGHTON PAPERBACKS

LIGHT A PENNY CANDLE

MAEVE BINCHY

'The most enchanting book I have read since
GONE WITH THE WIND'
Sunday Telegraph

'Compassionate, and delightful, this is the
magnificent story of twenty turbulent years in the
lives of two women. One is English, the other is Irish.
Their friendship is sealed when they are children: it
is warm, devoted, unshakeable and, against all odds,
it survives. Their names are Aisling and Elizabeth . . .

'Thank heavens – a thoroughly enjoyable and
readable book'
The Times

'Brilliant: a remarkable, panoramic and vastly
entertaining novel'
Molly Keane, Irish Press

'A marvellous first novel which combines those rare
talents of storytelling and memorable writing'
Jeffrey Archer

HODDER AND STOUGHTON PAPERBACKS

CHRISTOPHER BURNS

THE CONDITION OF ICE

In 1936 Ernest Tinnion leaves England for Switzerland to climb, with his childhood friend Hansi Kirchner, the awesome north face of the Versücherin. As they prepare the ascent, unforeseen pressures mount: from Tinnion's lover, who has left her husband to join him; from a too curious, menacing German photographer; and from a rival Italian team. In a breathtaking climax, Tinnion is forced to weigh survival against loyalty, neutrality against love and friendship, and to recognise ominous parallels with the looming global conflict.

'Christopher Burns' harsh, beautiful novel employs a number of unforgettable mountaineering images to dig deep into the condition of the European soul on the eve of the war'
Kazuo Ishiguro in The Sunday Times 'Books of the Year'

'Put Burns' imagination on a perpendicular cliff of stratified black rock with the cracks filling with snow and he'll have you feeling for a toe-hold in the carpet'
Nicholas Shrimpton in the Independent on Sunday

'Excellent, exquisitely crafted . . . One of Britain's finest writers has written a gripping, many-layered story'
Val Hennessy in the Daily Mail

'That rare thing: a novel of action and emotion which is also a novel about the way people think . . . it is a tremendous achievement'
D. J. Taylor in The Independent

CHRISTOPHER BURNS

THE FLINT BED

Eking out a solitary existence as warden of a Cumbrian nature reserve, Maurice Fretwell, a former priest, seeks sanctuary from his loss of faith. But when an American and his adopted Vietnamese daughter arrive, Maurice becomes unwillingly involved in their search for her natural parents, and the ensuing tragedy forces him to confront the past before regeneration can begin.

'Gripping on a narrative level, the book is also a powerful evocation of a bleak, monumental landscape in which humans slither about on their devious business'
Michael Dibdin in The Observer

'A chilling study of a well-intentioned man prised out of seclusion to confront a reality he can only deny – until it is too late . . . exactly why and how are mysteries that keep the narrative tense with expectation'
Judy Cooke in The Guardian

'The most haunting novel I have read this year . . . His themes are huge: the Vietnam war, immigration, the place of the priest and religion in modern society, the pain of lost faith, the obsessive love that can grow between father and daughter'
Jane Gardam in The London Evening Standard

'A considerable novelist. The characters are excellently done, the evocation of mood admirable; the prose is lucid and expressive'
Allan Massie in The Scotsman

'A haunting and compelling novel'
Kazuo Ishiguro in the Daily Telegraph

MORE TITLES AVAILABLE FROM
HODDER AND STOUGHTON PAPERBACKS

All these books are available at your local bookshop or newsagent, or can be ordered direct from the publisher. Just tick the titles you want and fill in the form below.

Prices and availability subject to change without notice.

HODDER AND STOUGHTON PAPERBACKS, P.O. Box 11, Falmouth, Cornwall.

Please send cheque or postal order for the value of the book, and add the following for postage and packing:

UK including BFPO – £1.00 for one book, plus 50p for the second book, and 30p for each additional book ordered up to a £3.00 maximum.

OVERSEAS, INCLUDING EIRE – £2.00 for the first book, plus £1.00 for the second book, and 50p for each additional book ordered. OR Please debit this amount from my Access/Visa Card (delete as appropriate).

Card Number ☐☐☐☐☐☐☐☐☐☐☐☐☐☐☐☐☐☐

AMOUNT £..........................

EXPIRY DATE ....

SIGNED ....

NAME ....

ADDRESS ....

....